Marry Luke for the sake of her reputation?

"I believe you, Beth." Luke inhaled deeply, then expelled a long, slow breath. "Except I don't know if everyone else will see it that way. They might find Millie's version more. . . interesting and that's not good. The Christians in this town wanted a schoolteacher above reproach."

"Oh, Luke, I'm sorry. . ."

"Well, there is one thing we can do."

She turned abruptly. "What's that?"

"It'll shut the mouths of the gossipmongers, no doubt about it." He stood and came forward, pausing just a foot away. "You'll be able to teach school come fall and no one will have a single qualm about sending children into your classroom."

Looking up into his suntanned face, she saw the twinkle in his blue eyes. "Luke? What do you have in mind?"

He smiled. "We can get married."

ANDREA BOESHAAR was born and raised in Milwaukee, Wisconsin. Married for twenty years, she and her husband Daniel have three adult sons. Andrea has been writing for over fourteen years, but writing exclusively for the Christian market for seven. Writing is something she loves to share, as well as help others develop. Visit Andrea's website at: http://members.aol.com/akbwrites2.

HEARTSONG PRESENTS

Books under the pen name Andrea Shaar
HP79—An Unwilling Warrior

Books by Andrea Boeshaar
HP188—An Uncertain Heart
HP238—Annie's Song
HP270—Promise Me Forever
HP279—An Unexpected Love
HP301—Second Time Around
HP342—The Haven of Rest

An Undaunted Faith

Andrea Boeshaar

Heartsong Presents

To Kathleen Rose Smith, Patricia Wolf, and
Margaret Been—thanks for the years of encouragement!

And special thanks to Alison Dingeldein for answering
my many questions about Arizona history and
Native American culture .

A note from the author:
I love to hear from my readers! You may correspond with me
by writing: **Andrea Boeshaar**
Author Relations
PO Box 719
Uhrichsville, OH 44683

ISBN 1-57748-703-6

AN UNDAUNTED FAITH

All Scripture quotations are taken from the Authorized King
James Version of the Bible.

Cover illustration by Randy Hamblin.

PRINTED IN THE U.S.A.

prologue

I, Bethany Leanne Stafford, am writing in a leather-bound journal my dear mother gave me before I left Milwaukee, Wisconsin. She suggested I write my memoirs of my impending journey west and my new life as a schoolteacher in the wild Arizona Territory.

To date, however, nothing exciting has occurred. We arrived in Independence, Missouri, where we have gathered our supplies for our trip. Pastor Luke McCabe (not to be confused with his father, the elder Pastor McCabe) said we will follow the Santa Fe Trail along with other migrants—most of them families. I am ever so excited about my impending adventure, although Mrs. Gretchen Schlyterhaus has warned me on more than one occasion that this will not be as comfortable as our train ride into Independence. Traveling by oxen-drawn covered wagons may undoubtedly prove to be a hardship, but both she and I are ready and eager to face each new challenge. Presently, we are waiting for more wagons to join our caravan. Due to the threat of Indian attack, the United States Army has forbidden us to proceed until one hundred wagons are collected for the journey. It may be a while before we are able to get started.

Journal Entry: December 27, 1866

I will never forget Christmas Day on the trail. Pastor Luke preached a wonderful message on Christ's birth and then we celebrated the best we could with what we had. We were almost able to forget our hardships along the way—

and we have had many.

One remains foremost in my mind: my first encounter with a rattlesnake. (On the farm in Wisconsin, I never saw anything larger than a pine snake, and pine snakes are not poisonous.) I happened upon the deadly reptile quite accidentally as I unloaded our wagon one evening. I nearly stepped on the horrid thing, and it poised, ready to strike me. In that fraction of a second, I knew I was going to die, but Pastor Luke saw the snake the same time I did. He managed to pull out his rifle and shoot it before it attacked me.

Afterwards, I just stood there, gazing at the creature's lifeless black eyes. Then I burst into tears. Pastor Luke put his hand on my shoulder. "There, now, Miss Stafford, that buzzworm's dead as a doornail. He can't hurt you anymore."

I am smiling as I write this, because Pastor Luke is the most unconventional minister I have ever met. His speech is a casual drawl and sounds nothing like the formal Eastern accent of our pastor back home. Furthermore, I cannot envision our refined Milwaukee pastor taking aim and shooting a "buzzworm." But Pastor Luke saved my very life that day, and I thank God for him.

Journal Entry: December 29, 1866

Yesterday a horrible thing happened involving another rattlesnake, but this time it resulted in a tragedy. A little boy named Justin McMurray got bit. His passing was the saddest thing I ever witnessed. He was only five years old.

Evidently, he was bit during the day, but his parents didn't realize it until our caravan stopped early that evening. Several men and one doctor went by the McMurray wagon to see if they could be of help, but it was too late. The poison had gotten into the boy's system and he had a fever.

Then Pastor Luke went over and talked to Justin, insisting I come along. When we arrived, my heart immediately went out to Mrs. McMurray. She looked so pained and helpless, but she held her child tight while his life slipped away with each passing second. He was coherent, despite the fever and chills, and he did not seem to be in too much pain, except for the arm where the snake had bit him.

Instinctively, I put my arm around Mrs. McMurray's shoulders in effort to comfort her while Pastor Luke talked to the boy about Heaven. He said, "Justin, do you know Jesus?" When the child shook his head, Pastor Luke explained about how Jesus died for everyone because we have all done wrong—even five-year-old boys. But Jesus lived a perfect life because He is the Son of God and so He took our punishment on the cross.

Justin listened intently as Pastor Luke clarified things in a way a little boy could understand. Soon Justin decided he wanted to pray and ask Jesus into his heart so he could go to Heaven. It was the sweetest prayer. He said, "Jesus, please forgive me for my sins and save me so I can come and play with You in Your big house in the sky." He paused before adding, "But Jesus, can I take my mama with me?"

I choked back a sob and glanced at Mrs. McMurray who had fat tears rolling down her cheeks. Pastor Luke's eyes looked misty, too, but instead of weeping, he started singing. He knew so many songs about rejoicing in Heaven that Mrs. McMurray smiled, and Justin even laughed a couple of times.

Finally the Lord took him home. I was so happy Justin was in the Savior's arms, but I felt a bit sick inside. I still do.

Journal Entry: January 18, 1867

For almost two weeks after little Justin McMurray's death, I kept dreaming awful things at night and could not sleep well. Each time I dozed, I would envision rattlesnakes everywhere—in the wagon, even in my hair! I would awake with a start, and Mrs. Schlyterhaus would hush me, since we both sleep inside the wagon, while Pastor Luke makes his bed below us.

My fear of rattlesnakes began to grow to the point where I refused to get down from the wagon and stretch my legs during the day, and at night I begged Mrs. Schlyterhaus to start the fire and make supper. I did not have any appetite, and at night I would lie inside the wagon and pray for some peaceful sleep. . .which never seemed to come.

One evening, Pastor Luke said, "Bethany Stafford, you climb down off that wagon." I told him I would do no such thing. He asked me why, but I could not get myself to admit how afraid I was to leave the wagon and have a rattlesnake kill me. However, Mrs. Schlyterhaus had apparently discussed my nightmares with him, because Pastor Luke guessed the trouble. He said, "There's no snakes around, so come down now or I'll climb up and get you myself." Still, I refused, but I tried to be polite about it. Next thing I know, Pastor Luke has his arm around my waist and was lifting me out of the wagon. Then he announced we were taking a stroll around the encampment.

I begged to stay back, but he would not be dissuaded. I went so far as to threaten him, saying if I died of snakebite, it would be all his fault. He said, "I'll take my chances." So I pleaded with him to at least carry along his rifle, to which Pastor Luke replied, "No, ma'am, we're only taking the Lord with us tonight."

My fear increased so much that my heart pounded and my legs shook with every step. Finally, Pastor Luke said folks were going to get the wrong impression about us if I did not begin to walk in a ladylike fashion. To my shame, I realized I was stepping all over him in order to get myself off the ground and away from the rattlesnakes I knew lurked beneath the sands of the Cimarron.

Pastor Luke's voice became very soft and gentle. He said, "Miss Stafford, God does not give us the spirit of fear, so don't be afraid. Do you think our Almighty Creator doesn't control the appointed hour of your death or mine? Of course He does. He is in control, and He will not take you home until His time is right."

I knew Pastor Luke spoke the truth, and somehow his straightforwardness made me relax. Then he mentioned what a nice evening it was and for the first time I realized he was correct about that, too. The sky looked clear and the air felt cool and clean against my face. Amazingly, I even felt hungry. I loosened the death grip I had around his elbow, and Pastor Luke chuckled as though he were amused. I felt horribly embarrassed, and he laughed again. Moments later, he asked if he could call me by my given name. After considering the request, I told him he could. It is a funny thing, but I did not fret about rattlesnakes the rest of the night.

Journal Entry: January 28, 1867

After fourteen exhausting miles a day for two months, we have finally arrived in Santa Fe. It is not at all like Milwaukee. Most houses are single-story adobe structures with dirt floors. Sadly, I am bone-thin and the traveling dresses I made for the journey hang from my shoulders like old potato sacks. Luke said he is worried about me, and so we will remain here for several weeks while I regain my strength.

We escaped bad weather for the most part, but we did encounter a buffalo stampede, the likes I hope to never witness again! We saw abandoned wagons and fresh graves, which proved to be an eerie forewarning. Days later, a strange fever made its way around our wagon train, and several people died, including four small children. Luke gave an encouraging grave-side message, but leaving the little bodies of their children behind was more than the three young mothers could bear. They wept for days, and my heart broke right along with them.

Luke soon enlisted my services, and he said I was a blessing to the mourning women. I prayed with them and helped them with their daily chores. As I helped them, oddly enough, my own heart began to heal.

Then I nursed Mrs. Schlyterhaus back to health, as she took ill with the fever as well. Luke said he didn't know what he would have done without me, but I really did not do that much.

As for Mrs. Schlyterhaus, Luke has decided that although her health is improving, she will remain here in Santa Fe permanently. He has arranged for her to stay with a missionary family and work as their housekeeper. Mrs. Schlyterhaus is very accepting of this arrangement. She said the thought of another four weeks traveling through Indian territory frightens her senseless.

In truth, it frightens me a little also. But, as Luke is fond of saying, God does not give us the spirit of fear and, from the human standpoint, he has taken precautions to ensure our safety. He hired a guide—a physician named Frank Bandy, one of the few white men who has made peace with the Apaches. The Indians allow him passage through their territory because he has been able to medically minister to their people.

But, alas, I must stop writing for now as there are numerous tasks I would like to accomplish—although if Luke discovers I am not resting, I may have some explaining to do.

Journal Entry: June 15, 1867

I have discovered I keep a poor journal. Truth is, I forgot about my diary these past months. However, this morning I shall do my best to bring the events up to date.

We arrived in Silverstone a little more than a month ago. I seem to have fully recovered from my journey, and now I spend much of my time becoming familiar with my surroundings and the people here.

The Arizona heat is ghastly and I doubt I shall ever get used to it. I find myself looking forward to my cool baths every morning at the break of dawn, when several of us women go down to the river bank, as is the custom of the Mexican women here. The muddy water looks red and the river's current is swift; however, the coolness is a welcomed respite.

Silverstone is located north of Arizona City on the Colorado River. The scenery is breathtakingly beautiful, the majestic mountaintops seem to touch an ever-azure sky, and the red river swirls beneath them. But the town is an eyesore by comparison. It's an unpainted freight town but a necessary channel for getting supplies up from Tucson and Arizona City and over the mountains to Prescott, the territorial capital. The people here are a mix of prospectors, ranchers, freighters, Mexicans, and Indians. They keep Main Street (if it may be called such a thing) lively.

On one side of the rutted, unpaved road is an adobe government building that houses the sheriff and a jail, a saloon, and a "house of ill-repute," as Mrs. Baker calls it. On the other side of Main Street is Bakers' Boarding House (in which I am presently residing). The Bakers also operate a restaurant and the post office. Next to their place is a dry-goods store, and a freight office, where Pastor Jacob works when he is not preaching. At the end of the thoroughfare is the church and the small, one-room school where I will be teaching in the fall.

As one might guess, the two sides of Main Street are largely at odds with each other. Mrs. Baker says we are the "good" side and those across the way are the "bad" side—all save for Sheriff Paden Montano, of course.

Luke informed me the sheriff has been commissioned by the United States Army and oversees the shipping and receiving of the government freight brought to Silverstone by river steamers. Then the goods are transported across the Territory by wagon. Mrs. Baker's fourteen-year-old daughter Millie said Sheriff Montano's father was a rugged vaquero and his mother was a genteel woman from back East. The sheriff seems to have inherited traits from both parents. He is a darkly handsome man with hair so long it hangs nearly to his waist. At first glance, one would assume he is an Indian since he looks quite fearsome. Like his vaquero father, he is a capable horseman and masterful with a gun. Like his mother, by whom he was raised, he is well educated. Some say Sheriff Montano is a Mexican and Indian sympathizer, out to use his status as a United States lawman for his own purposes, but Luke says he's a fair man. I must admit I have found the sheriff to be charming.

And then there is Ralph Ames who is quite the opposite. He is a Christian, but he can still be quite disagreeable. His wife died during childbirth just before we arrived in town, and Mr. Ames is desperately trying to replace her as he would a mule. I was insulted when he proposed to me, for I find his philosophy on marriage highly distasteful. But I do pity his eight darling children. I have enjoyed taking my turns mothering them, although I am not interested in marrying their father and I told him so.

In truth, my plans do not include marriage. I am here to be a teacher. I decided that much before I ever left Milwaukee. After my atrocious experiences with men last summer, the details of which I shall never print, I have resigned myself to becoming an old maid.

When I mentioned this to Luke, during our discussion of Mr. Ames' proposal, he laughed good and hard. Then he said, "Beth, if you die an old maid, I will be sorely disappointed."

I did not know what he meant, but his expression made me blush. Sometimes Luke worries me with the things he says. . . .

one

Bethany set down the quill and capped the inkwell. Closing her journal, she stood from where she'd been sitting at the rough-hewn desk Mr. Baker had hammered together for her use just as a knock sounded at the door. Then, without waiting for a reply, Millie Baker poked her round cherubic face into Bethany's bedroom.

"Mama says breakfast is ready."

"Thank you, Millie, I'll be down shortly."

The flaxen-haired girl grinned. "Pastor Luke and Pastor Jacob are already here. Sheriff Montano, too."

"Oh?"

"Yes. Three handsome men all together in the same room. Why, they could set a girl's head to spinning."

Bethany felt her irritation rising. The fourteen-year-old was as bouncy as a rubber ball, but she was becoming a shameful flirt!

"Who do you think is more handsome, Miss Stafford?" Millie prattled on. "Pastor Luke, Pastor Jacob, or the sheriff?" She stepped into the room and closed the door behind her. A conspiratorial expression spread across her face. "I fancy the sheriff, even though he's not a Christian. Although he might convert some day. Only God knows." Her wide blue eyes grew dreamy. "Paden Montano is a handsome curiosity, is he not?"

"I don't notice such things," Bethany fibbed, folding her arms in front of her. If truth be told, only a woman deaf and blind wouldn't notice Paden Montano; however, she wasn't about to encourage Millie. The young lady would be one of her pupils this fall, and Bethany wanted to set a good example. "And what would your parents have to say if they heard you talking like this?"

Millie shot a glance at Bethany. "You're not going to tell them, are you?"

Bethany raised a contemplative brow. "Well, maybe not this time. But you must stop allowing your thoughts to be consumed by romance. You're going to get hurt."

"Pshaw!"

"Millie, really!"

The girl was unabashed. "Miss Stafford, if you haven't already noticed, you and I are the only eligible women in Silverstone! We can have our pick of any man we want."

"You are not eligible," Bethany replied, knowing the Bakers wanted their only child to receive an education before she married. "And I am not. . .interested."

"Are you certain about that?" Millie taunted. "You and Pastor Luke seem to spend a lot of time together."

Bethany's cheeks flamed with embarrassment and aggravation. "Millie, I'm a teacher and Pastor Luke—and Pastor Jacob, I might add—are starting a school. It's only natural that we'd spend time together. . .to plan and organize."

"Well, fine. But I am interested—in getting me a husband!"

"You're much too young."

"Am not! My friend, Martha, got married last year. . .and she's younger than me!"

"Than I," Bethany corrected. "And every circumstance is different. Perhaps Martha was more. . .prepared for marriage than you are."

"I'm not a child!" Millie pouted and stamped her plump foot. "Why do you and my parents treat me like one?"

Bethany couldn't hold back a grin. Millie Baker frequently behaved like a child—and one given to temper tantrums at that! Little wonder everyone thought of her as such.

But in spite of the vexation the girl caused her, Bethany was determined to be her friend and trusted teacher. Perhaps she'd somehow make a difference in Millie's young life. However, she certainly wouldn't accomplish such a feat by arguing with her.

Turning, Bethany peered into the looking glass, thankful it had survived the journey west. Once it had occupied the far corner of her bedroom at home, but now it stood beside an unfinished wardrobe.

Bethany smoothed down the skirt of her calico dress. In the past few weeks she'd put on some weight, so her clothes fit nicely once more. In fact, they were almost snug. She made a mental note to purchase some material and make a few new dresses, and a new camisole and chemise, too.

"I'm famished," she announced, changing the subject. "What has your mother made for breakfast?"

Millie's face brightened. "Oh! She cooked up the most delicious-smelling omelets with Spanish tomatoes, peppers, and onions. . .and biscuits, of course." She looked thoughtful. "Ever wonder why men insist upon biscuits at nearly every meal?"

Bethany laughed lightly. "I suppose the biscuits help satisfy their voracious appetites." She took Millie's arm. "Come along. Let's go downstairs."

They strolled amicably to the stairway. "Aren't you the least bit interested in getting married, Miss Stafford?" Millie asked.

Bethany paused in the hallway as a vision of Luke McCabe flitted through her mind. Marrying him was not at all an unpleasant thought. But she quickly squelched the idea. It wouldn't do to fall in love with him, only to discover he didn't return her affections. She had lived through that heartache twice already.

While growing up on a farm in Milwaukee, Wisconsin, Bethany had always assumed she'd marry their neighbor, Richard Navis. Her father had even led her to believe she and Richard would eventually marry. But then last summer Luke's sister Sarah came to town. She was a music teacher, working as an interim governess for Captain Kyle Sinclair, a wealthy shipping entrepreneur. One thing led to another, and soon Richard fell head over heels in love with her—and eventually Sarah loved him, too, leaving Bethany heartbroken and embarrassed. The truth emerged; Richard hadn't ever loved her, except as a sister in Christ.

Trying to overcome his rejection, Bethany gave her heart away once more, this time to Lionel Barnes, who proved to be a shameful philanderer. He proposed marriage, and she accepted, but before long she learned she wasn't the first young woman Lionel had used for his amusement. When she refused to allow him certain liberties, Lionel admitted he didn't love her and broke their betrothal. Once again, Bethany felt dejected and ashamed.

She inhaled deeply now, thanking God that Luke showed up when he had, needing a schoolteacher in the Arizona Territory. Initially, he had wanted his "baby sister" Sarah to take the position, but since she set her sights on marrying Richard, Luke abandoned that idea and pursued Bethany as a possible candidate. Things worked out, and here she was.

And now she could make a new start. She had left her past heartaches behind in a different part of the country, another world away. She harbored no ill feelings toward Richard and Sarah; in fact, she considered the pair her good friends. She had even forgiven Lionel. She was ready to forget the past and go on. But if she ever married, it would be to a man who loved her so much he couldn't see straight, a man intoxicated with love for her. Of course such a man did not exist, so she put the notion out of her head. She would focus on her teaching position instead.

Turning to Millie, Bethany attempted to answer the girl's question. "I guess I'd be a liar if I said I never wanted to get married. Doesn't every woman? But I've learned other things in life are more important. For instance, serving others, showing them the love of Christ. . ."

"Yes. I think so, too."

Bethany felt hopeful as they began descending the stairs. So she was making a difference with Millie. How wonderful!

Just then, the girl tugged at her arm. "I think you and Pastor Luke are well-suited. Are you just a tiny bit interested in him?"

Bethany swallowed a retort. So much for being influential. Millie flounced into the dining room of the boardinghouse, and Bethany watched in dismay as she boldly approached the sheriff and began a conversation.

The girl was certain to get her heart broken. Bethany sensed it coming like a brewing thunderstorm off in the distance. The men in Silverstone were not exactly refined gentlemen with whom a young lady could trifle in the parlor. No, they were hard-working river men, vaqueros, former soldiers—and when it came to their land, their horses, and their women, these men were serious.

"Well, good mornin', Beth."

Startled out of her thoughts, she looked up and found Luke leaning against the banister. His rakish smile didn't seem to belong on a pastor's face.

" 'Morning, Luke."

"You look right pretty today," he drawled. "Can I escort you over to the dining table?"

"Yes, thank you."

She tamped down her sudden uneasiness. Millie was right: She and Luke did spend a lot of time together. Moreover, his compliments made her uncomfortable, mostly because she couldn't get herself to believe they were true. Bethany knew she was plain, plain as a field mouse. Her hair was a nondescript brown and hung nearly to her waist, though more often than not, she pinned it up at her nape. Her eyes were an average bluish-gray, like the sky on a misty morning, and her lips were just an ordinary shape. A smattering of freckles covered her nose and cheeks—her own fault, since she abhorred wearing a bonnet. All in all, she wasn't anything special.

Just plain.

So why was Luke behaving as though he. . .cared? He certainly couldn't be attracted to her.

But of course, Luke would care a little, just as he would have cared about Sarah had she been the one to come out West. After all, he'd taken great pains to get her out here to teach school. Besides, Bethany reminded herself, Luke had promised her father that he'd protect her.

While Bethany considered him through lowered lashes, Luke slipped her hand around his elbow and guided her toward the dining room. He was nearly ten years her senior and about the most handsome man she'd ever laid eyes on. His hair was the color of wet sand, and his blue eyes were as clear and inviting as a cool lake on a hot summer day. A shadow of perpetual whiskers along his well-defined jaw line made the good pastor appear more like a shady outlaw; however, his warm and friendly smile disarmed even the worst skeptics. His tall frame included broad shoulders, slim hips, and long legs, and on many a Sunday morning, Bethany found herself admiring God's messenger instead of listening to his message. But she'd gotten over that silliness now. She simply refused to look at Luke while he preached and instead forced herself to listen closely while she fixed her gaze on her Bible.

Bethany smiled inwardly, recalling a past conversation with Sarah McCabe Navis. Just before she'd left Milwaukee, Bethany confessed to Sarah that her brother Luke was so handsome he made her nervous. At the same time, though, she had vowed never to give her heart away. Not to Luke. Not to anyone. Instead, she'd promised to throw all her energy into being the best schoolteacher Silverstone had ever known.

They reached the dining table, and Luke seated her politely before taking his place beside her. The other men in the room nodded to her.

"Good morning, Miz Stafford."

She smiled and inclined her head cordially. "Sheriff Montano." Turning to Jacob, she greeted him also.

Like his younger brother, Jacob was tall and blond, but where Luke's eyes were blue, Jacob's were brown. Having met all the McCabes, first at Sarah and Richard's wedding, then at their home just outside of St. Louis, Missouri, Bethany had quickly noticed how much the entire family resembled each other. And where the two McCabe sisters, Leah and Sarah, were lovely, their three brothers were equally as handsome.

While everyone else took their places, Bethany allowed her gaze to wander around the table. She was surprised to find Paden Montano eyeing her with interest. She shifted uncomfortably and lowered her chin, studying the plate in front of her.

"You look very rested, Miz Stafford," the sheriff said. Bethany found his soft Mexican accent enchanting. If she were completely honest, she'd have to agree with Millie: Paden Montano was definitely a "handsome curiosity." Today his shiny, dark hair had been pulled straight back and tied with a piece of leather string. His tan skin looked clean-shaven with the exception of his sleek, black mustache. "I trust you are finding your stay here in Silverstone quite comfortable," he added, his dark eyes shining like polished stones.

"Yes, I am, Sheriff," she replied demurely. "Thank you."

"Well, let's ask God's blessing on the food and dig in," Mr. Baker suggested from the head of the table. "Pastor Jacob, will you do the honors?"

"Of course." Jake smiled and glanced around the table. "Let's pray." He bowed his head and said a few simple words of thanks. Then dishes were passed around the table.

"So, Paden, I hear you had some excitement last night," Ed Baker said, forking a large piece of egg into his mouth.

"Excitement, indeed. Cattle rustlers hit the Buchanan ranch. Clayt suspects the Indians, of course."

"Any truth to that?" Ed smacked his thick lips together beneath his long, bushy, light brown beard. "I heard there's a tribe living just over the eastern ridge."

"*Sí*, but they are a very civilized band. They're not bloodthirsty, nor are they interested in the Buchanans' cattle."

Sheriff Montano took a long drink of his coffee. He smiled at Doris Baker. "Ahh, a good strong brew. Just the way I like it."

The older woman blushed. "I'll be sure to tell Rosalinda," she promised, referring to the grandmotherly Mexican cook.

"About that looting last night, Paden," Ed continued, "you think us townfolk have to worry?"

"No."

"Well, what are you going to do about it?"

"Watch. Keep my ears open." The sheriff paused to chew his food and then sat back in his chair. "I have a hunch it is the work of outlaws, but they will not get away."

Millie sighed dreamily. "You're so brave."

He gave her an indulgent smile.

"Well, I'd keep my eye on them Redskins, if I was you," Ed remarked. "Can't trust them. I just wish the government would hurry up and take care of them."

Paden Montano's face was devoid of expression, although his next words were deliberate and carried force. "It is a shame that most people feel as you do, Ed, because I have known many an Indian to be more trustworthy than a white man." He looked over at Luke. "I'm sure the pastors would agree. God made the Indian as well as the white man. Isn't that right?"

"He did."

Ed snorted. "Well, even God makes mistakes."

"No, sir, He does not," Jacob quickly replied. Leaning back in his chair, he folded his arms. Bethany could tell he enjoyed the turn in the conversation. "The God of the Bible is perfect and does not err. He made people in His image. 'For God so loved the world that he gave his only begotten Son, that whosoever believeth in him should not perish but have everlasting life.' I reckon the words 'world' and 'whosoever' includes Indians, Mexicans, and every other kind of people there is."

"Thank you for the sermon. And it ain't even Sunday."

"Oh, now, Ed," Doris admonished her husband. "Birds fly and pastors preach."

Next to Bethany, Luke chuckled. "Amen!"

Paden's mustache twitched slightly. Then he slid his chair backward, scraping its legs against the wooden plank floor. "If it is any consolation, Ed," he said, adjusting his gun belt as he rose, "I have every intention of finding those cattle rustlers, whoever they are, and I gave Clayt my word."

The man nodded in satisfaction.

Turning to Doris, Paden added, "Breakfast was delicious, as always. Please compliment Rosalinda for me."

"I shall. Thank you, Sheriff."

With one last nod in Bethany's direction, the sheriff strode purposely for the door, leaving a starry-eyed Millie Baker gazing after him.

Bethany expelled a weary sigh. Would she ever be able to convince the girl to look beyond her romantic fantasies before she got hurt?

Just then Ralph Ames burst into the building. He wore a determined expression that skirted on desperation, and Bethany felt a twinge of anxiety. No doubt the man had come to ask for her hand in marriage once more, and, no doubt, she'd have to turn him down. . .again. Yet she did pity the man and his difficult circumstance. No wife and all those children. . .

" 'Scuse me, Miss Stafford," Ralph began breathlessly, "but I need to speak with you. And, Preacher," he added, his gaze hardening and moving to Luke, "I'll thank you to stay out of this!"

two

Luke rose from his chair. "Well, good mornin' to you, too, Ralph," he drawled, wearing an amused grin.

"I mean it, Preacher. I come here to speak with Miss Stafford—privately. So mind yer own business!"

All humor slipped from Luke's expression. "Miss Stafford is my business."

Jacob stood and cleared his throat. "Oh, now, brother, I don't think it'll do any harm if Ralph has a word with Bethany," he said diplomatically. "Provided, of course, she's willing to talk to him."

When Bethany glanced up at Luke, she found his blue eyes staring back at her, his golden brows raised in question. "It's all right," she replied, though she was deeply embarrassed to be the center of such heated attention. "I'll speak to Mr. Ames." Turning to the man, she added, "Shall we talk over there? In the lobby?"

"Yeah, I reckon that's all right," he muttered, casting Luke one more resentful look.

When they reached the lobby, which really wasn't anything more but a small extension of the dining room, Ralph continued his grumbling. "I'm so tired of that man poking his nose into my affairs. This here's between you and me, nothing to do with him."

"Mr. Ames, he's merely protecting me. My father is back in Wisconsin and he trusted Luke to bring me out here to teach school."

Ralph rubbed his stubbled jaw line. "Ain't got nothing to do with protection. It's just plain selfishness."

Bethany inhaled sharply at the remark.

"And that brings me to the reason for my visit. I need a

22

wife," he blurted. "My children need a mama. The Bakers told me their daughter is too young to wed, and I reckon they're right. She ain't much older than my girl. The Widow Stevens turned me down, so yer the only one left."

How utterly romantic, Bethany thought wryly, looking into Ralph's wooden brown eyes. His face wasn't unpleasant, just unkempt, and she felt certain he could be a handsome man if he tried to take care of himself.

But therein lay the problem: Ralph Ames seemed to have no desire to take care of anything that belonged to him. Bethany had witnessed the man's negligence firsthand when it came to his children, and she'd heard he had mistreated his wife.

"Don't you realize God brought you out here so you could take care of my family?" he continued. "I prayed about this and I'm sure yer supposed to be the mama of my younguns."

"But—"

"Now, submit yerself to God's will, Miss Stafford."

"But I don't believe it is God's will that I marry you," she countered.

"Well, that's where yer just going to have to trust me."

"No, Mr. Ames. I'm sorry, but I cannot marry you."

"Why not?"

"Because I didn't come to Arizona to get married. I came here to teach school."

"So school my children. There's eight of 'em. Why, you can have your very own schoolhouse after you marry me."

Bethany turned and paced several steps away. Perhaps if she tried brutal honesty this time Ralph would listen to her.

"Mr. Ames," she said, turning back around. "There's another reason I can't marry you." She swallowed hard. "I don't love you."

"Well, I don't love you either," he retorted.

His words cut to the core of Bethany's soul. Entering into a loveless marriage went against everything she'd ever dreamed or longed for in this world. She'd rather die an old maid than spend the rest of her life with a man who didn't love her.

"Now, look, Miss Stafford. Out here, you marry when it's convenient. . .or if there's a need. Be reasonable. Think of my children. Can you deny them a mama? Someone to care for them?"

"They are being cared for." She refused to allow herself to be cowed by this man. "Women from the church, myself included, are giving their time to help with the children and the chores around your house. Mrs. Canton is feeding your baby and seeing to his needs. The only time you're required to care for your family is in the evening, after supper is made and the dishes are washed, and. . .well, you'd have to do that even if you had a wife, for pity sake!"

Ames' grizzled jaw dropped in obvious surprise at her outspokenness, but Bethany was undaunted. "Your children need to spend time with you. There are things only a father can teach his offspring. And as for God's will, I have prayed about marrying you. If God led me to do so, I would obey Him. But that is not the case."

"What are you saying?"

Bethany groaned with frustration. "I am saying, that I will not marry you—now or ever!"

His gaze narrowed. "Know what you are? Yer a little upstart, that's what. There's rebellion written all over yer face, and I'd wager you wouldn't know God's will if you tripped over it." Angrily turning on his heel, he paused near the dining table where everyone else still sat, looking unnaturally stiff. "Some kind of schoolteacher you picked for us, Pastor Luke. Pretty soon our children will be rising up against us on account of her. You should've hired a man like I said." Throwing Bethany one more irate glance, he stormed from the boardinghouse.

Mrs. Baker stood and marched toward Bethany. She looked quite militant, Bethany thought, with broad shoulders and her silvery-blond hair pulled back tightly. "Don't you dare listen to a thing that man says!" She pulled Bethany into a motherly embrace. "Why, Ralph Ames ran his poor dear wife into the ground and now he's looking for another workhorse."

"Oh, now, Doris." Mr. Baker twisted around in his chair. "Ralph is a good man. He was kind to Elizabeth."

"Kind as prickly pear, you mean," she retorted. "Why, he made his poor sick wife get up and feed the horses after Doc Ramsey ordered her to stay in bed." Doris shook her head. "The gall of that man! And poor Elizabeth. . .she was so worried about delivering a healthy baby with no thought for herself." She whispered to Bethany, "Doc Ramsey said she bled to death on account of the fact she didn't rest. And wouldn't it just figure—Ralph refused to name little Michael. Left it up to Margaret Canton. Pitiful, isn't it?" With an arm around her shoulders, Doris walked Bethany back to the table. "And Margaret told me Ralph has no interest in his newborn son, which puts a strain on the Cantons, of course, seeing they've got six children of their own."

Bethany sat down, unsure of whether she felt better or worse. Perhaps her forthrightness to Ralph Ames would put an end to any further marriage proposals. But she did feel badly for his children and the Cantons.

"Bethany, I apologize," Jacob put in. "Had I known what Ralph wanted to say this morning, I'd have shut my mouth and let Luke here take care of him."

Bethany caught Luke throwing his older sibling an I-told-you-so look.

"Sorry 'bout that," Jacob reiterated.

"It's quite all right," she murmured.

"So, what are your plans today, brother?" Jacob asked, obviously pleased to change the subject.

"I promised Harlan I'd help him at his ranch, seeing his arm is still broken." A lopsided smile spread across Luke's face. "He's another one who didn't listen to Doc Ramsey."

"Men are sure stubborn." Doris dabbed the corners of her mouth with her napkin. "And they're as thickheaded as oxen."

"Why, thank you for the compliment, ma'am," Luke replied amusedly.

Everyone chuckled while Doris blushed. "Oh, now, I wasn't talking about the men in this room," she explained. "I was just thinking of men in general."

Luke leaned over to Bethany. "I can recall a few stubborn women myself," he said quietly. "Do you remember that day on the trail when Mrs. Smith refused to cross the Canadian River on account of being scared to death of drowning?" He grinned. "The river stood only two feet high in that particular spot."

Bethany smiled. She remembered.

"No whispering, you two," Millie reprimanded them. "If y'all have something to say, tell everyone. That's what Mama taught me. Right, Mama?"

"That's right," she said as Rosalinda began clearing dishes from the table.

"Very true," Bethany conceded. "Whispering at the supper table is quite rude." She exchanged guilty glances with Luke.

He turned to Millie. "Reckon I started it. My apologies, Miss Millie."

"I forgive you both."

In spite of herself, Bethany looked over at Luke again and laughed softly. The sudden vision of poor Mrs. Smith and the veritable fit she threw all the way across the river suddenly seemed so funny. Of course, it wasn't at the time, and if she and Luke shared the story, it most likely wouldn't be amusing to anyone else. It was just another of the many moments of understanding she and Luke seemed to share. But Bethany refused to think too hard about it. If she did, she might end up falling in love with Luke McCabe. . .and then she would get her heart broken a third time.

"I believe I'm finished with breakfast," Bethany announced firmly, before her tumultuous emotions could get the best of her. She picked up her plate and followed Rosalinda out into the kitchen.

The hot Arizona sunshine beat down on Luke as he and Jacob walked back to their quarters behind the church. The day promised to be a scorcher and he almost wished he hadn't committed himself to working out on Harlan Whitaker's ranch beneath the blistering sun.

"You know, brother," Jacob began, "there's been some speculating on you and our new schoolteacher. Truth is, I've done a bit of speculating myself."

"Well," Luke drawled, "I told you Beth had my interest piqued ever since we left Wisconsin. She was so shy and melancholy at first, it was a challenge for me to even make her smile. When I succeeded, I felt like a prospector who'd just found gold! Still do."

"So? You going to ask her to marry you?"

"Maybe."

Luke's gut tightened at the very thought. He had no problem confronting a man about the eternal destination of his soul; however, when it came to asking a woman to marry him. . .well, that was another story. He didn't think he could abide a rejection like the one he'd had from Suzanna James back in Missouri when he was nineteen years old. He'd been infatuated with Suzanna something terrible, and her refusal had kept him a bachelor the last seven years.

But lately. . .lately he'd been seriously considering the idea of marriage again. And Bethany Stafford was the reason his thoughts continued along those lines. There was just something about her, and he'd been praying and asking the Lord to direct his paths in this matter. So far, God had shown him her courage more than once on the trail. Yet other times Bethany seemed as vulnerable as a small, gray-eyed kitten. Maybe her youthful innocence made him want to protect her, share his life with her.

Did she want the same?

Occasionally, Luke suspected she had feelings for him, judging by the way she gazed up at him with something akin to adoration in her eyes. But would she marry him—or would she turn him down like she had Ralph Ames?

"You scared?" Jacob goaded him.

"You bet!" Luke nodded and tipped his wide brimmed hat to Mrs. Hensley as she passed by on the boardwalk. "Beth told me she came out West to teach school, not get married."

"Well, you could change her mind with a little charm."

Luke cast his brother a furtive glance.

Jake laughed. "Seriously, I think you'd better propose marriage to her before someone else gets to her first. Like the good sheriff."

"He's not a believer, Jake. Bethany wouldn't marry a nonbeliever." Luke paused before adding, "I wouldn't let her!"

"Well, you know what they say about the love of a good woman. Haven't you seen the way Montano's face lights up with interest when Bethany enters the room?"

Luke didn't reply, but he'd seen it all right. "He's most likely intrigued with Beth because she's the only woman around who doesn't swoon over his good looks."

Jacob grinned. "Now, I'd be inclined to think that remark stemmed from sour grapes on your part, brother, except I've taken note of it myself. Bethany Stafford doesn't bat a single lash at the debonair Paden Montano."

"Aw, he ain't so debonair. And where'd you learn that word, anyway? You sound like Valerie."

Jacob chuckled. "Can't say I learned it from our sister-in-law, although she is forever using those fancy French words."

They shared a laugh, and Luke recalled the day their oldest brother, Benjamin, had up and married a dark-haired, blue-eyed Southern belle from New Orleans. That had been six years ago, not long after the battle at Bull Run that started the War Between the States.

"Well, I think you'd better decide whether you're going to marry Miss Bethany Stafford," Jacob said as they reached their destination, "or else stand aside and let other fellows have a chance at her hand."

Luke nodded although the thought of "other fellows" put a knot in his chest.

"Once God revealed that Grace was the woman for me," his older brother continued, "I didn't waste a single moment before proposing."

"Yeah, I remember. You rode into Arizona City posthaste after breakfast one day and asked her to marry you." Lifting a brow, Luke continued, "You're just lucky Grace waited around for you. You've known each other since grade school and she's been crazy about you all this while. She even followed you out here!"

"I thought she wanted to put her nursing skills to good use in Arizona City. Reckon I was pretty oblivious to her feelings," Jacob admitted. "But no more. By the way, did I tell you that Grace's cousin Catherine is coming to the Territory? Traveling by stage. Should be here in a few weeks to help Grace with wedding plans."

"Catherine Elliot. . .no fooling? She's coming out here?" Luke shook his head. "I haven't seen that woman in years."

"Let me remind you, brother, that her last name is Harrison now. She married shortly after Ben and Valerie. Just such a shame that her husband Stephen died in the war."

"I heard about that tragedy when I was home. Mama said Catherine was devastated."

"She was—but she's healing."

"Good."

"But let's not stray too far from the subject," Jacob said. "What about Bethany?"

Luke grimaced. "I don't know."

"Couldn't hurt to at least court her."

"No, I s'pose it wouldn't." Inside the cabin, as Luke collected a few things he'd need today, he thought he might prefer the blazing sun on Harlan's range to any kind of rejection from Bethany. Turning to his brother, he added, "We'll see."

three

Luke paused on the ridge to appreciate the sight before him. Harlan Whitaker's ranch spread out as far as the eye could see, his crops to the east, while cattle dotted the western edge. Luke suddenly longed for his own homestead, but he quickly reminded himself that covetousness was a sin. Old Harlan deserved his acreage. After all, he had been one of the few settlers who'd stayed on after the army pulled out when the Civil War erupted. Most ranchers left their homesteads on account of the renegade Indians who were known for their thieving and murdering of not only whites but other tribes as well. However, Harlan refused to leave his land, even though it had cost him the lives of his oldest son and scores of field hands.

"Sure appreciate yer ridin' out here today, Preacher," the aging man told Luke as they met just inside the Whitaker property line. His dark, thinning hair was hidden beneath a red and white checkered bandanna, topped with a wide-brimmed hat. Leaning forward in his saddle, he added, "Hard to find good help these days."

Luke grinned in spite of himself. Rumor was a man took his life into his own hands when he set out to work for Harlan.

"Hope yer a good shot." Glancing at Luke's waist, he frowned. "No holster. . .gun? Are you crazy?"

"I don't carry a gun on me," Luke drawled, unaffected by the insult. Harlan wasn't the first to wonder if he was *loco*. However, Luke did pack a Winchester .44 Carbine in his saddle just in case he came face to face with a wild boar, snake, or sundry other nasty critters. He'd shoot them in a minute. But a human being—never. Never again. Luke had made a vow at the end of the war that he'd never take another human life, even if it was in self-defense. He'd rather die than kill another living soul.

"Now, Preacher," Harlan insisted, "you'll hafta carry a gun today. Just take one look at my hogs and you'll see why." Turning his horse, he led Luke around to the far side of his ranch and stopped near the hog pen. "Will ya look at that? And don't laugh, Preacher. It ain't funny!"

Too late. Luke chuckled at the sight. There before his eyes were hogs all right, but several had arrows protruding from their thick skin, and they squealed loudly as they circled the pen.

"My wife says they look like four-legged pin cushions."

"I'd say that's about right."

Harlan shifted in his saddle. "Indians come by almost ever'-day and shoot arrows into my hogs. Then I've gotta butcher 'em. Guess there's another thing you can help me with later today. Now, about that gun. . .you can use one of mine."

"No, thanks, friend," Luke said with a confident grin. "My God is bigger than all the Indians put together."

"Yer a fool."

Luke let the ridicule blow on by like the hot, dusty, desert wind. He'd made his decision and he wouldn't go back on it no matter what anyone else might think.

"Well, I reckon I'll put you in the barn. You can repair a few harnesses. Can't rightly send you out on the range, seeing as yer being so mule-headed."

"Harlan, you want me on the range, that's where I'll go, gun or no gun."

"You got suicide on your brain this morning, Preacher? You can't ride the range unarmed."

Luke shrugged. "Choice is yours."

Harlan thought it over, then slapped his hat onto his receding brown hair. "I reckon I got enough men out minding the cattle. You go on over to the barn."

"Sure thing."

After tethering his horse, Luke walked into the barn, thanking God he'd work out of the sun most of the day. As he breathed the scent of dried grass, sweat, leather, and horses, his eyes slowly adjusted to the darkness of the rough-hewn building. Damaged harnesses hung from large nails on the wall; Luke pulled one down, inspected it, and got to work.

Hours later something at the doorway caused the barn to grow unnaturally dim. Luke looked up and barely glimpsed a man's silhouette before a shiny object came hurling toward him. Luke tripped backward just as the blade whizzed by him, lodging itself in the splintering wall. Then an Indian brave stepped inside the barn.

Luke didn't utter a sound as he stared at the expressionless face framed by long black hair. His gaze moved downward from the brave's long-sleeved white tunic, belted with ammunition, to his sun-bleached britches tucked into leather knee-high moccasins. In the Indian's left arm, he cradled a rifle that Luke recognized as an old Henry .44 and suddenly he wished he'd taken Harlan's advice and packed a pistol. But oddly, a sense of peace soon enveloped his being.

The brave took another cautious step forward, eyeing Luke as intensely as Luke had scrutinized him. Finally, he said in broken English, "You no have gun."

Luke shook his head. "No. No gun."

The Indian's dark gaze narrowed, and then he tipped his head in speculation before glancing over his shoulder warily. "Me kill you, White Man."

"Yeah, I reckon that's the plan."

The warrior seemed perplexed by the quip, and again he looked over his shoulder. "Why you no have gun?"

"Don't need it." Luke glanced upward. "My God protects me."

The brave followed Luke's line of vision and studied the roof of the barn. At last, he pointed to it. "Your God?"

Luke grinned. "No, no, that is not my God. My God is the God of the Bible who lives in Heaven."

Understanding washed over the warrior's face. "Ha! Your God not protect you from my gun!" He shook his rifle under Luke's nose.

"No, but if you kill me, I will be with my God in Heaven."

The other man frowned, and his jaw dropped in wonder.

"My God loves all people," Luke continued, figuring his time was short and he'd best get as much evangelizing in as he could before meeting his Savior. "He loves Red Men just as much as White Men. My God sees no difference between you and me."

The tip of the rifle was suddenly thrust into his throat. "White Men murder my people," the Indian sneered.

"And Red Men murder my people. Can't we stop killing each other and live in peace?" Luke's eyes met the warrior's gaze. "Peace."

Slowly, the gun lowered from his throat.

"Hey, Preacher. . .?"

The brave jumped and cocked his rifle, pointing it toward the door. Luke put his hand on the barrel. "No need for killing," he whispered. Then, persuading the warrior back into a dark corner, Luke touched a finger to his lips, urging his uninvited guest to remain silent.

"Yeah, Harlan, go ahead."

"Anita's about got supper on the table," he hollered, "and she don't want you eating with the hired hands on account of you being a man of the cloth and all."

Luke's gaze never left the Indian's. "I appreciate that. Tell your wife I'll be along shortly. Just finishing up in here."

"Very good." The sound of Harlan's retreating footsteps echoed inside the barn.

For a long while the two men stared at each other. Finally, the brave said, "You Preacher?"

Luke nodded. "Name's Luke McCabe."

"Preacherlukemccabe," the other man said as if the three names were all one word. "Me, Warring Spirit." He thumped his chest.

Luke smiled; the name fit. "I wish you peace, Warring Spirit. Peace that comes from the one, true Living God."

Warring Spirit's dark eyes narrowed before he turned and left the barn, vanishing as quickly as he'd appeared.

❧

After surviving his encounter with Warring Spirit, Luke felt unusually courageous as he rode into Silverstone. So when he learned Bethany was still in the schoolhouse, he decided to pay her a visit. But deciding he smelled about as ripe as a Missouri cornfield during planting season, he adjusted his plans to include a quick dip in the cool Colorado River.

"I'm back," he announced, entering the tiny cabin he shared with his brother, "and I'm taking a swim."

Looking up from the books scattered across the scarred, plank tabletop, Jacob grinned. "I imagine you deserve it, out on the range all day."

"Actually, I was indoors all morning, making repairs. Then I helped Harlan butcher hogs. But I met an Indian brave just the same."

Jacob sat back, wearing an expression of interest, and folded his arms. "You don't say. . .?"

"Yep. And it's only by the grace of God that I'm alive to tell about it."

"Well, hallelujah!"

"Hand me that soap, will you?"

Jacob twisted around in his chair and grabbed the strong-smelling bar, then tossed it in Luke's direction. "Since when do you need soap for swimming?"

"Since I decided to court Miss Bethany Stafford—starting tonight."

Jacob let loose with a loud "Whoo-wee!"

"Pipe down," Luke said irritably. "She's liable to hear you in the schoolhouse next door—and I'm liable to lose my nerve."

With that he left the cabin, his brother's chortles following him all the way down to the river bank.

four

Bethany loved to read just about anything she could get her hands on and, consequently, she became so engrossed in the novel she'd found that she didn't hear Luke enter the one-room schoolhouse. Only when he finally cleared his throat did she look up from her book. Standing, she tried to hide it in the folds of her skirt.

"Luke. . .I didn't hear you come in."

"Hello, Beth." He stepped forward, smiling, his eyebrows raised. "What are you reading?"

She grimaced, realizing he'd seen the book. "It's one of the books Mrs. Buchanan donated to the school this afternoon. Look at all of this, Luke!" She waved her hand at the crates cluttering the plank floor. "Mrs. Buchanan said she loves books and has dozens of them shipped from San Francisco twice a year. These are just some she felt she could part with."

Luke's gaze traveled quickly over the wooden containers before it came back around to hers. "That's mighty generous."

Bethany nodded, and Luke stepped closer until he stood right in front of her. Then he held out his hand.

"Let me see what book's got you so captivated."

Guiltily, she relinquished the novel.

Luke inspected it. "Hm. . .*Mountain Mary.*" He raised his blond brows. "A Dime Novel, Beth?"

"I'm doing research," she said in her own defense. "You see, my mother never allowed these books in our home, so I wanted to see what the fuss is all about. . .in case one of my students has a penchant for these things. I wouldn't want to be ignorant."

"I should say not." Luke grinned and handed back the

novel. "And just what is all the fuss about?"

"Well, in this particular story, Mountain Mary is quite a fearsome lady. She can tackle a bear and fend off an entire band of Indians singlehandedly. Except, she's willing to give up her love of the mountains for the love of her life. . . quite the sacrifice for her."

Luke smirked. "Sounds unrealistic, if you ask me."

"Yes, I must confess it is. But the story is very compelling."

"I imagine so, from what I saw when I walked in." He took a seat on the corner of the long table at the front of the room and smiled. "Did you have a good day?"

She nodded. "I stayed busy. I helped Millie with the mail earlier." Her expression fell. "Nothing from home yet."

"It takes a while, Beth, and more often than not, letters get lost along the way."

"I know. I guess I'm just feeling. . .well. . ."

"Homesick?"

Nibbling her lower lip, Bethany thought it over. "No, not homesick. Just. . .out of touch with the world."

Luke laughed. "Welcome to the Wild West."

She rolled her eyes and set *Mountain Mary* on a stack of books. "Oh! I almost forgot—do you know what Mrs. Buchanan told me?"

"No, what?"

"Her husband Clayton, along with their son Matt, are planning to take the law into their own hands and find the cattle rustlers who looted their ranch. I mentioned it to Mr. Baker, and he seemed to side with the Buchanans. They think the Indians are the thieves, but I rather believe Sheriff Montano's theory."

Luke's smile broadened. "You sure are getting to be a spunky little thing."

Bethany folded her hands in front of her and sighed deeply, regretfully. She hated to think she'd embarrass Luke in any way. "That's not a good thing, is it? Spunk? I should really be more docile, shouldn't I?"

"No, you shouldn't," he assured her. "A woman needs to have some gumption out here. Although," he added, grinning, "Mountain Mary is a bit extreme."

"All right." Bethany smiled. "I'll stop wrestling bears in my free time." As she stooped to pry open another crate of books, she heard Luke's deep laugh.

When she looked up at him, she thought he seemed awfully clean for having been on a ranch all day. His blond hair was parted neatly to one side, his cotton jeans seemed as crisp as the tan shirt he wore. *Must have important business somewhere this evening,* she decided.

One by one, two by two, she began lining up the books so she could tell Mr. Baker how big a bookshelf she'd need. After all, the man enjoyed pounding furniture together, crude as it could be at times, and Bethany wasn't about to rob him of his fun. "How was your day, Luke?"

"Quite interesting. I met an Indian by the name of Warring Spirit. Snuck up on me while I was in Harlan's barn. He said he planned to kill me, though now that I think it over, I suspect he only meant to intimidate me. It worked. I figured I was going to die."

"Oh, Luke!" Bethany felt horrified at the very idea.

A smile tugged at the corners of his mouth. "Would you miss me, Beth, if I'd have gotten killed this afternoon?"

"What kind of question is that?" Flustered, she turned her back on him and set down another armful of books. Why would he ask her such a thing? But his steady silence made her realize he was actually waiting for an answer. "Of course I'd miss you," she said quickly. "The whole town would miss you. If you were dead, Luke, who would preach to us on Sunday mornings while Pastor Jacob rode his circuit?"

She picked up another book, opened it, and pretended to be suddenly very interested in its subject. *Why does he say such things to me?* she wondered. *He says I look pretty, asks if I'd miss him. . .doesn't he know a girl could get the wrong idea?*

"It's a nice evening, Beth. Care to take a stroll?"

Turning on her heel, she gaped at the man. A stroll? Slowly it dawned on her that Luke was just treating her as he might his younger sister. Except she wasn't his sister, and the things he said were affecting her heart in a most unreasonable way.

"You know, Luke. . . ," she began, intending to be straight-forward with him. She fingered the edge of the book nervously. "For the better part of a month now I've been meaning to tell you something, but it's hard to say."

"You're interested in a young man here in town?"

"Interested?" She shook her head. "No."

"That's good."

She huffed in mild aggravation. He'd done it again! "Luke McCabe, if you talk to all women the way you talk to me, you're bound to have some angry husbands on your hands. Women just naturally take to those niceties. . .those compliments."

"Yeah," he drawled, watching her carefully, "I reckon they do. But I don't flatter all women."

"Just your sisters."

"Well, I suppose—"

"But I'm not your sister, Luke. I'm not even a relation."

"For which I am most thankful," he said emphatically, wearing a wry grin.

Bethany, however, refused to be deterred by his smart remarks. She simply had to explain so he'd understand once and for all. But this morning's confrontation with Mr. Ames had left her with the impression that men were thickheaded when it came to feminine reasoning. Once more, she'd have to be blunt.

"The way you've been behaving causes me to wonder if you're interested in me. . .romantically. . .which I know is not the case," she added hastily. "And, just for your information, my mind has not been saturated with Dime Novels. I'm merely stating the facts from a woman's point of view. For your own good."

Luke blinked. "I see."

She nodded. Judging from his expression, she knew he understood.

"But what if I am interested, Beth?" The sudden earnest expression on his face made him look almost vulnerable.

"Interested. . .?" The word seemed to stick in her throat. "In me? Why?"

He smiled gently. "How 'bout we go for that stroll? It's awful stuffy in here."

Before she could reply, he stood, took her elbow and propelled her toward the open doorway. They descended the steps of the schoolhouse, and then, much to Bethany's astonishment, he looped her hand over the crook of his arm.

Was she dreaming? Had she imagined the last few minutes of conversation?

"You know, I think it's going to rain," he said easily.

Bethany didn't reply. She felt dazed.

They stepped onto the boardwalk and passed the general store, Luke keeping a slow pace so Bethany could keep up with his long-legged strides. "I heard a druggist from California has plans to set up shop right here in Silverstone."

"Yes, I'd heard that, too." She began to relax.

"Now that the war is over, I imagine more folks will be coming out west. Those moving into California will likely cross the river at the Yuma Crossing, which means additional business for Silverstone, seeing as our town is right on the way."

Bethany agreed. "Mr. Baker said much the same thing. He's even talking about opening a hotel."

"Is that so? What do you think he'll do with his boarding-house?"

"Run it just as he is now, I would guess."

"Hm. . ."

The last of Bethany's tension slowly receded, and she began to enjoy strolling along beside Luke this way. All too soon they arrived at the Bakers' place.

"I think I'll say good night here. Don't worry about the schoolhouse. I'll close up for you on my way home."

"Thank you."

"I'll see you tomorrow at breakfast. . .perhaps we can talk some afterwards."

She managed a polite nod, but inside her emotions were reeling.

Luke smiled. "Well, g'night." There was a softness in his blue eyes that made Bethany's face flame, although she managed to bid him good night.

Then she entered the boardinghouse and closed the door behind her. As she leaned against it, she realized too late that she'd walked in on some sort of meeting. The lobby was filled with men, and a thin layer of gray smoke from their tobacco swirled near the ceiling. Her presence went unnoticed, for all eyes were riveted on the red-haired man on the stairway.

"This here's a call to arms, men," he shouted. "Our families are at stake. Them Indians gotta be stopped. The government isn't doing its job, so we've got to take matters into our own hands."

Shouts of enthusiasm filled the room.

"Cattle rustling is a high crime, one that can't be allowed to go unpunished. If we let those savages get away with stealing our livestock, there'll be no telling what they take next. Might even be our wives and children."

The audience murmured in concern.

"So, are you with me?"

Bethany winced as loud affirmations filled her ears.

"Then, as soon as it's dark, we ride!"

More cheering broke out and Bethany slipped back out the door. The sun was sinking amid ribbons of orange, red, and lavender clouds, but she barely noticed. *I must do something.* She nibbled her lower lip in indecision. *If I don't, innocent lives might be lost!*

She spied the sheriff's office farther down Main Street

and took off in a run for that direction. Just as she reached the end of the building and prepared to cross the thoroughfare, someone grabbed her roughly around the waist. She tried to scream, but a gloved hand went over her mouth as she was half carried, half dragged around to the back of the boardinghouse.

"Miz Stafford," a low husky voice said close to her ear as the iron-like arm tightened around her, "are you trying to get yourself killed?"

five

Bethany relaxed as she recognized Paden Montano's deep, smooth voice. Slowly, he lifted his leather glove from her mouth and she whirled to face him.

"Sheriff, I was just on my way over to see you!"

He smiled down at her, a curious look in his eyes. "Is that so?"

She nodded, growing uncomfortable as Paden's dark gaze boldly assessed her face, lingering on her lips, while his muscled arm still held her captive. Bethany could feel the top of his ammunition belt press against her ribs, and she hoped no one would happen to pass by and see them in this most compromising position. Placin her hands against Paden's black leather vest, she tried in vain to push more distance between them.

"And what were you coming to see me about, Miz Stafford?"

"I need to tell you something. . .ooh! Let me go!"

Abruptly, Paden released her and Bethany would have fallen backward had he not caught her elbow.

"I apologize for apprehending you that way—but the alternative would have resulted in your being run over by twenty exuberant cowboys on their way out of the boardinghouse." He raised his swarthy brows. "But you have my undivided attention now, I assure you. What did you want to see me about?"

Pulling out of his grasp, Bethany gave him a quelling look. "Those same men, the ones you claim would have run me over. . .well, I overheard their discussion tonight." With an effort, she collected her wits. "They're planning to ride—"

"I know all about their intentions," Paden cut in, his expression stony.

42

"But, the Indians. . .they plan to kill them. And you said the Indians are a civilized band and innocent of cattle rustling."

"That is true. And I am aware of tonight's plans. But you, Miz Stafford, should not go about eavesdropping."

Bethany lifted her chin. "I was not eavesdropping! I simply walked into the boardinghouse and there they were!"

"Mm." The sheriff's expression was both amused and patronizing.

"Oh, never mind!" Why ever did she think this man was charming?

"Miz Stafford?"

She looked over her shoulder.

"Forgive me, *chiquita*. I appreciate your concern. Very few would care if Indians were murdered."

"I don't want anyone to be killed."

"I know. You are a very special young woman."

Bethany gave him a skeptical look. "What are you going to do?"

Paden smiled tolerantly. "I will try to persuade the men of this unlawful posse to turn back and allow me to take care of finding the real thieves. After that, what more can I do?"

"Will they listen?"

He shrugged.

"But you're one man against so many."

"I will do what I can. Meanwhile, you mustn't worry your pretty head about such things. Go on inside." Paden nodded toward the back entrance of Bakers' boardinghouse. "I can still hear excitement in the voices coming from the front. It would not be wise for you to meet up with those ruffians right now."

The sheriff's dark eyes seemed to plead with her and Bethany felt she had no other choice but to comply with his wishes.

"Very well," she acquiesced. "Good night, Sheriff."

Removing his wide-brimmed hat, he bowed. "Sleep well, Miz Stafford."

❧

That evening, kneeling beside her bed, Bethany petitioned the Lord for Paden Montano's safety when he confronted the angry mob of men. She also prayed about her conversation with Luke, scarcely believing that he could have taken a romantic interest in her. She entreated her Savior for wisdom for the school year. "And please bless Mama, Papa, Billy, Jonathan, Julia, Eliza, and little Ned," she finished. "Oh! how I miss my brothers and sisters. Bless Sarah and Richard and all the Navises as well as the McCabes. And please, Lord, keep me safe in this untamed land."

She got off her knees, then lay down on her bed in the hot, airless room. Bethany knew in her heart that God had heard her, yet she couldn't help feeling He was as far away from her as her family and friends back home in Wisconsin. Every night, she struggled to read her Bible, but the verses failed to hold her attention. She couldn't figure out why. She loved to read! Why not God's Word? Oh, she waded through it and some passages stuck in her mind—but the Scriptures didn't seem to take root in her heart.

I've got no business entertaining thoughts of becoming a pastor's wife, she mused, turning onto her side and watching the moonlight stream through the window's muslin curtain. *Certainly there's someone else more qualified for Luke.*

Oddly, though, the thought of him marrying another woman saddened her. She wished she could turn off her feelings altogether and just stay busy, concentrating on one task at a time.

Of course, the Dime Novel she'd been reading hadn't helped matters. And neither had Paden Montano's earlier behavior. She'd never had a man hold her so tightly before and she found herself imagining Luke's arms around her instead of the sheriff's, Luke's lips close to hers. . .

She stopped herself. Foolish girl! She closed her eyes and tried to fall asleep, but her thoughts crowded her mind, loud and demanding. Finally, when the first pinks of dawn lit up the eastern sky, she drifted off into a fitful slumber.

❧

"I saw it with my own two eyes!" Millie declared to everyone in the dining room of the boardinghouse. Her parents as well as Jacob and Luke McCabe stared at her.

"Are you sure?" Ed looked aghast.

"Positive. It was Miss Stafford and Sheriff Montano. They were out back last evening. I watched them from my window. He had his arms around her. Why, I'll bet he was whispering all sorts of romantic things 'cause Miss Stafford looked like she was about to swoon!"

"Mercy!" Doris exclaimed. "A shameless tryst."

Ed turned to Luke. "Pastor?"

"I'll talk to Bethany. I'm sure there's some reasonable explanation." Luke certainly hoped so, anyway.

"I can't imagine what it could be," Ed replied sternly. "My daughter's not one to go making up stories."

"I'm sure she's not." Luke gazed at Millie, noticing she refused to meet his eye. Her chin dropped guiltily, and he breathed an audible sigh of relief, thinking the girl had fabricated the whole tale. "Let me remind everyone in this room," he began, "that bearing false witness against another believer is a serious offense."

"Oh, I'm not bearing false witness, Pastor Luke," Millie said with an earnest expression. Her fat, blond curls swung with every shake of her head. "It's true about Miss Stafford and the sheriff. They were out back and he had his arms around her and—"

"All right, that's enough." Luke held up his hands, forestalling further details. He couldn't bear to hear anymore, now that he suddenly believed Millie was relaying the facts.

At that moment, Bethany descended the stairwell. All eyes turned toward her, and a look of confusion flitted across her face.

"Good morning," she said hesitantly. "Am I late?"

The stares from the others continued, and she looked down

self-consciously at her brown skirt, then glanced behind her, up the stairwell. Luke nearly chuckled.

He cleared his throat. " 'Scuse us," he said, getting to his feet. "Beth and I are going to have a. . .conversation."

She looked at him askance, her eyes filled with questions.

"Shall I hold breakfast?" Doris asked.

"No, ma'am," Luke said over his shoulder. "Y'all go on and enjoy your meal." Taking Bethany by the elbow, he escorted her out of the boardinghouse.

"What's going on?" she demanded as they began walking down the rough boardwalk that ran along the storefronts on Main Street. The sky was gray, and the smell of rain hung in the air like an imminent threat.

"Why don't you tell me."

"Tell you? Tell you what?" She looked up in his face. "Are you angry?"

He stopped walking and looked down at her. "Should I be?"

"I don't know. . . ."

They resumed their stroll, the tension mounting between them. Finally, when they reached an intersection, Luke steered her down a wheel-rutted road where Bethany hadn't ventured before. With each step, they left Silverstone farther behind.

"I'd like to hear your version of what took place last night," Luke finally said as they came to the end of the road. A craggy bluff plunged downward into a rocky valley. Luke took a seat on one of the flat, red stones on the ridge, well away from the edge of the cliff, and motioned for Bethany to sit on the ledge across from him.

"Last night?" She looked confused.

Luke got right to the point. "Millie said she saw you and Sheriff Montano last night, engaged in a. . .well, let's call it an intimate discussion."

Bethany gasped. "She saw us?"

"Aw, Beth." Luke winced. "So it's true?"

"Well, yes. . .sort of. . ."

"But I asked if you were interested in someone yesterday when we spoke in the schoolhouse, remember? Why couldn't you be honest with me?"

"But I'm not interested in Sheriff Montano!"

"Millie said he had his arms around you."

"Yes, but. . ." She shook her head vigorously. "Luke, this isn't what you think. Please let me explain."

He nodded curtly, and Bethany relayed the entire event, beginning with the meeting in the boardinghouse. She told Luke how she'd left to inform the sheriff of the plans she'd overheard, and how Sheriff Montano had grabbed her off the street. "You see," she concluded, "the sheriff was merely taking me out of harm's way."

Luke wasn't pacified. "I think it's a whole lot more on his part." He raised a hand, preventing further argument. "But I believe you, Beth." He inhaled deeply, then expelled a long, slow breath. "Except I don't know if everyone else will see it that way. They might find Millie's version more. . .interesting, and that's not good. The Christians in this town wanted a schoolteacher above reproach."

"Oh, Luke, I'm sorry."

"It's not your fault," he relented.

"Perhaps Sheriff Montano will agree to explain," she suggested hopefully.

"Perhaps. Unfortunately, he's not sheriff of this town on account of his impeccable character. He's a fast draw, and he communicates well with the Indians. He's also unafraid to deal with outlaws. But he's no saint."

"You once told me he's a fair man. Surely everyone in town agrees."

"For the most part. But is that enough to save your reputation from the town gossips?"

The question was a rhetorical one, and Bethany knew it. She felt so awful for disappointing Luke this way. He and Jacob had worked hard to gain the trust of the people in

Silverstone. They were seen as men who grew their congregation by leading others to the Lord, not by making false promises or accepting bribes. Folks respected the McCabe brothers. However, this scandal was sure to disgrace them, Luke especially.

Standing, Bethany walked a few steps away, kicking the gravel aimlessly.

"Well, there is one thing we can do."

She turned abruptly. "What's that?"

"It'll shut the mouths of the gossipmongers, no doubt about it." He stood and came forward, pausing just a foot away. "You'll be able to teach school come fall and no one will have a single qualm about sending children into your classroom.

Looking up into his suntanned face, she saw the twinkle in his blue eyes. "Luke? What do you have in mind?"

He smiled. "We can get married."

six

"Well, that was the shortest courtship I ever saw!" Jacob declared later that morning. "Twelve hours. . .and you slept through six of them!"

Luke grinned, his gaze roving around the little cabin where they now sat. Small but efficient, the rough-hewn building provided easy access to both the church and schoolhouse. He felt certain that with a little imagination Bethany would get this place feeling like a home. A table and four chairs occupied a good amount of space on one side, and the stone hearth had been built into the middle of the far wall. Two wooden beds with straw mattresses had been set up in the back corner, but pushed together, Luke decided they'd accommodate a newly married couple just fine.

His smile widened as he looked back at his older brother. "So, when did you say you're moving out?"

"I didn't." Jacob lifted an indignant brow. "When did you say you're getting married?"

"As soon as you'll conduct the ceremony. How's this afternoon sound?"

"You never were a patient man," Jacob grumbled. "But you're going to have to wait a spell this time. Grace and I aren't getting married till the end of the summer, and it won't be till then that we make our home in Arizona City and begin church planting. Besides, you best allow Bethany to come to her senses. Why, that girl looked thunderstruck when you two came back to the boardinghouse and made the announcement."

"No, Jake, you don't understand," Luke countered teasingly. "I want to marry Beth *before* she comes to her senses."

They shared a chuckle, but Luke knew his brother was

right. He'd have to give Beth some time to adjust to the idea of becoming his wife.

His wife. The thought suited him just fine, and he'd never been in favor of long engagements.

"We could have a double wedding," Luke suggested.

Jacob shrugged. "I'll ask Grace what she thinks."

"Worked nicely for Sarah. You should have been there."

"Wish I was."

"I never thought I'd see the day our baby sister would get married." Luke grinned, thinking back on the event. He recalled how fetching Bethany looked at the reception in her simple rose-colored gown. She was so shy at first that he could barely wheedle two words from her mouth. But the trek west seemed to have cured her bashfulness. Unfortunately, it'd been replaced by a mettle that could make a man's head whirl. "How'd I ever think she was plain?"

"Who, Sarah? Sarah's not plain. Pa used to have to fend off her admirers with a stick."

"Not Sarah. Bethany. When I first met her, I thought she was plain. That's one of the reasons I figured she'd make a good schoolteacher out here. . .I figured the men would let her be. I suppose she isn't beautiful by the world's standards—but there's something about her that makes her awfully attractive to me."

Jacob smiled wryly. "You sound like a man who's been bitten by true love. Say," he added, relaxing back in his chair, "you think her parents are going to want her to return to Wisconsin for the wedding?"

"I hope not." Luke rubbed his whisker-rough chin, then folded his arms over his chest. " 'Course, I'd best send a telegram, asking them permission to marry her. I reckon I'm doing this all backwards, although I suspect Mr. Stafford will give me his blessing."

"Need to go into Arizona City today? I'd be more than happy to accompany you."

Luke lifted an inquiring brow. "Looking for an excuse to

see Grace, huh?" The sheepish expression that flitted across his brother's features was answer enough. "Got plans today?"

"Nothing that can't be changed and rearranged. What about you?"

"I've got a couple of obligations, but they'll wait till tomorrow."

"Well, let's go." Jacob stood. "And you'd best plan on wiring Mama with the news or she's liable to tan your hide, all the way from St. Louis!"

Luke grabbed his hat. "Good thinkin', brother."

๛

Bethany felt as though she might scream if Millie didn't stop her rambling. And she still hadn't completely forgiven the silly girl for defaming her character before breakfast. But now Millie was stuck to Bethany's side, and the girl's excitement grated on her nerves.

"Oh! I just knew you and Pastor Luke were meant for each other! And to think you forced his hand by leading us all to believe you and the sheriff were romantically involved. How clever you are, Miss Stafford!" Millie sighed dreamily. "Pastor Luke is so in love with you that he couldn't bear the thought of you in Sheriff Montano's arms and he had to claim you for his own. Soon you'll be his wife."

"That's hardly the scenario," Bethany ground out, "and I'll thank you not to go repeating that nonsensical story." She paused before she could spill out the truth. Luke was marrying her to save her reputation in this small, dusty town, and love had nothing to do with it.

Her heart ached with that realization as she and Millie continued their stroll up Main Street toward the general store. A loveless marriage. The very thing she'd been determined to avoid.

Except she couldn't do better than marry Luke McCabe. Bethany had the utmost respect for him and. . .she had feelings for him, too. Now she could permit those feelings to grow into full-blown love for her fiancé. Perhaps if she loved him enough, he would, in time, return her affections. Hadn't he said last night that he was "interested"?

But interest wasn't the same as love. Of course she supposed she could approach him and ask, "Do you love me, Luke? Do you care?" However, the very idea of confronting him about such a particularly crucial matter of the heart caused Bethany a good deal of trepidation. She'd never been good at speaking her mind when her emotions got in the way.

"Oh! I'm so happy for you," Millie continued. "May I be in your wedding, Miss Stafford? I've never been in a wedding, not in my whole life!"

"We'll see," Bethany hedged. "I'm not certain of the details yet."

"I can't wait. I love weddings!" In all her exuberance, Millie fairly bounced down the warped boardwalk.

Bethany shivered in the light rain that fell from the overcast sky. She couldn't help but remember her previous engagement to Lionel Barnes and the heartbreak that followed it. Of course Luke wasn't anything like her former fiancé, but insecurity nagged at her all the same.

If only Luke loved her.

"And just think," Millie persisted, "Pastor Luke is on his way to Arizona City to wire your father and ask permission to marry you." Suddenly she stopped short.

"What is it, Millie?" Bethany paused as well.

"Your father won't deny his request, will he?"

"Probably not. He met Luke last summer and thinks very highly of him."

"That's good. Oh, Miss Stafford, we'd best get sewing on your wedding gown!"

Bethany groaned inwardly as they resumed walking. Then it dawned on her that soon she and her friend Sarah would be more than sisters in Christ. They'd be sisters-in-law! The idea brought a small smile to Bethany's lips. *I'll have to write Sarah and tell her. . .*

They entered the general store and were greeted by the proprietor's wife, Mrs. Scottsdale.

"Miss Stafford and Pastor Luke are betrothed!" Millie blurted. Bethany frowned. They weren't ready to announce it yet; they had to wait for her father's approval.

"Oh, how marvelous." The tall, thin woman's voice sounded sarcastic. Her dark brown hair was pulled back into a severe knot and her piercing ginger-colored eyes narrowed in scrutiny. "Do you still plan to teach in the fall?"

Bethany forced a smile and nodded.

"And what if you get in the family way?" Mrs. Scottsdale asked, peevishly. "Then what will we do? What will our children do? They won't have a teacher. We'll be right back to square one."

A heated blush spread across Bethany's cheeks. "Well, I. . . I guess we'll just have to trust the Lord to give me children in His timing."

"Hmpf," the woman snorted.

Bethany began inspecting the bolts of material set out in rows on a large table. She had plenty to choose from, thanks to the freighting that took place on the Colorado River. Silverstone wasn't as primitive as some towns in the Territory, though it wasn't as sophisticated as Arizona City. In any case, both towns were still recovering from the devastating blows inflicted upon them by the Civil War.

The tiny bell above the door jangled, signaling another patron's entrance. Millie gasped.

"Don't look now, Miss Stafford," she whispered loudly, "but it's one of the working girls from the brothel! Why, it's a wonder Mrs. Scottsdale allows her in here with other respectable customers."

"Her money is just as good as yours, Millie," Mrs. Scottsdale retorted. "My husband and I are in business, after all, and it's none of our concern where the funds originate."

"Yes, ma'am." Millie gave Bethany a dubious glance.

The "working girl" stepped farther into the store and began

quietly browsing at the next table. Bethany watched her curiously. The young woman didn't look much older than herself, with her flawless peaches-and-cream complexion and hair the color of golden honey. She looked up warily, and Bethany saw her sad, pale blue eyes.

Leaving Millie's side, Bethany strolled over to the next table with a boldness in her heart she'd never experienced before. "Hello, I'm Bethany Stafford," she began politely, "and I'm the new schoolteacher in town."

"I'm Angie Brown," the girl replied in a small, careful voice.

Millie inhaled sharply. "Miss Stafford, you ought not talk to her!"

"I'm just introducing myself," Bethany said over her shoulder. She turned back and gave Angie an apologetic grin.

"I'm telling Mama!" Millie ran out of the general store, leaving Mrs. Scottsdale frowning in her wake. The proprietress turned her glowering countenance on Bethany.

"You'd be wise to mind your own business, Miss Stafford," Angie warned softly. "You wouldn't want to lose your teaching position on account of me."

Bethany nodded reluctantly and returned to her task of selecting fabric. But all the while, she couldn't rid her mind of Angie's haunted eyes. At last, she made her purchases and left the store, grimacing at the thought of what Millie might be relaying to her mother.

seven

When Bethany returned to the boardinghouse, she fully expected a reprimand for speaking to Angie Brown. But to her surprise, the Bakers, including Millie, were so engrossed in conversation they scarcely noticed her entrance.

Eyeing the man they talked to, Bethany realized she'd never seen him before. His brown, shaggy hair framed a ruddy face, and he had the thin, wiry frame of a fifteen-year-old, though his eyes held a wild look that didn't belong to a man so young.

"You say it was an ambush, son?" Ed Baker asked gravely.

"Yes, sir. Twenty-two men were killed. Best as we can figure, someone tipped off the Indians." The young man paused, shaking his head sadly. "They were waiting for us." He gulped. "Only reason I survived was because my horse got killed and I managed to crawl beneath him and hide. No-good Redskins probably thought I was dead, too."

"What a shame!" Mrs. Baker declared.

"All those men dying. . .why, I'm going to cry for a week!" Millie exclaimed dramatically.

She sniffed loudly, and Bethany had to force herself not to roll her eyes heavenward at the theatrics. At the same time, Bethany's eyes stung at the news of so many deaths.

Doris Baker noticed her presence then. "Why, Bethany, did you hear? Some of Silverstone's finest men were murdered last night while performing their civil duties."

"Yes, I heard."

"Some are saying the sheriff informed the Indians," the young man stated, "but he's got an alibi—says he was at Chicago Joe's all night. One of the working girls backs up the story."

55

"Merciful heavens!" Doris exclaimed. "And here I thought that man had some scruples."

Bethany's reaction mirrored Mrs. Baker's, although she kept silent.

"But Mr. Buchanan swears he'll find the man who sided with the Indians and see that he hangs. Meanwhile, another ranch got raided last night and a field hand got killed—got an arrow right through the heart."

"Them Indians gotta go," Ed muttered. He looked down at the plank floor and shook his head in obvious disgust.

Doris walked over to the young man and looped a motherly arm around his drooping shoulders. "Come on over to the table and I'll have Rosalinda fix you up a good hot meal."

"Thank you, ma'am."

Millie bounced along in their wake. "All those men. . .all those handsome men dead. It just doesn't seem possible."

Bethany didn't know what to think. Was the sheriff really involved? Was his alibi a fabrication? On the other hand, she couldn't condemn him if he'd merely alerted the Indians. But was he directly responsible for the ambush?

She heard wagon wheels come to a halt outside the boardinghouse, and turned to see a man in a blue army uniform climb down from his perch. He grabbed a bundle from the back of the wagon and headed toward the boardinghouse. Once inside, he dropped the package on the floor.

"This here's some mail that should've got delivered yesterday. Came to Fort Yuma by mistake."

"Well, thank you," Doris said, with unmistakable crispness in her voice.

The soldier tipped his hat and left. Millie ran to the window and watched the man climb back up into the wagon.

"Oh, aren't those Union soldiers a handsome lot?"

"Millie!" Her mother looked horrified. "I will not have you ogling a Yankee!"

"Yes, Mama." The girl stepped away from the window, wearing a penitent expression.

"The war is over," Bethany stated. "There's no Union and Confederacy, just one United States Army."

"That's right, Mama," Millie said hopefully. "Could be that man was a Confederate. . .before the war."

"Quite unlikely." Bethany had never heard Doris use such an angry tone before. There was a moment of strained silence, and then the older woman seemed to snap out of whatever bothered her. Glancing at Bethany, she said, "I never did say congratulations on your engagement."

"Thank you." Bethany could still barely believe all that had happened in the last few hours. After a thoughtful moment, she added, "Mrs. Baker. . .about last night. Millie didn't lie, but it wasn't what it seemed. The sheriff and I were not meeting secretly. . .shamefully."

"Of course you weren't. I know that."

Bethany sighed with relief.

"Pastor Luke wouldn't have asked you to marry him if he thought you were a woman who carried on with a man in back of boardinghouses!"

Her relief quickly turned to disappointment as Bethany realized how right Luke had been about her reputation being soiled. She'd been redeemed in the Bakers' eyes now, but only because of his marriage proposal.

"Pastor Luke is one of the finest men I know," Doris continued. "If my son were alive today—" She swallowed hard, her usually jovial countenance masked by sorrow. "I'm certain that if my son hadn't been killed by Yankees, he would be as much a gentleman as either of the McCabes."

Bethany inhaled sharply. "I'm sorry. I didn't know."

"We don't speak of my son John's death often."

She nodded and suddenly Mrs. Baker's anger with the Union Army was understandable. "How tragic to lose a son in the war."

"Yes. . .but we cannot dwell on the past," Doris said firmly. "My son knew and loved the Lord Jesus. He is with Him today." After a deep breath, she looked at Bethany and her lips twitched. "Besides, we've got a wedding to plan!"

"Oh, please can I be in your wedding, Miss Stafford?" Millie began to plead again.

Bethany gave both women a weak smile. If only Luke had asked her to marry him because he loved her. . .

❧

Millie threw a veritable temper tantrum when her father ordered her to sort the mail. As a result, she was sent to her room for the remainder of the day, so Bethany volunteered for the task. She really didn't mind, for she hoped to discover a letter from home in the bundle the soldier had dropped off this morning.

Mr. Baker informed her that folks in Silverstone checked their mail bins whenever they came into town, so she created piles according to the names of the addressees. She noted that Sheriff Montano had received a couple of very official-looking envelopes, and soon she found a fat packet addressed to Pastor Jacob McCabe that appeared to be from St. Louis. Bethany was certain that would be a welcome surprise. But unfortunately, there wasn't anything for her. Picking up the very last letter, she hoped against hope it would be from her parents or Sarah; instead, the name read *Miss Angela Brown*.

Bethany bit her lower lip thoughtfully. Should she personally give Angie her mail? Mrs. Baker had warned her never to cross the street, so she couldn't very well knock on the front door of the brothel without causing quite a stir.

But what if she delivered the sheriff's mail and then slipped out the back door of his office? No one would see—and perhaps by doing this small favor for Miss Angela Brown, she would have a chance to share Jesus.

Her mind made up, Bethany gathered the mail. "I've got an errand to run," she called to Rosalinda who was dusting the furniture. "I'll be back shortly."

The Mexican woman nodded, and Bethany left the boardinghouse. Outside, the arid June day felt like an oven against her face. Would she ever get accustomed to the Arizona heat?

After several wagons rolled past, she crossed Main Street and quickly entered the sheriff's office. It was cool inside the adobe building, and once her eyes adjusted to the darkness, Bethany found Paden reclining lazily in his chair, his feet up on the desk.

"Miz Stafford," he drawled, "to what do I owe this unexpected pleasure?"

"No pleasure," she said. "I'm simply distributing your mail and I need to use your back door." She plopped his two letters on the desk and then strode purposefully past the jail and up a few wobbly wooden stairs to the back entrance.

"Hold it."

Bethany turned. "Yes, Sheriff?" she asked sweetly, fluttering her lashes ever so slightly.

He swung his booted feet off the desk and stood. As he walked slowly toward her, Bethany was reminded of a sleek black panther stalking its prey. He stopped just inches away. "What are you up to, *chiquita*?"

"I'm not doing anything against the law," she assured him. "I'm simply delivering a letter to Angie Brown."

Paden Montano raised an eyebrow. "Angie Brown? Who is that?"

Two steps up, Bethany stood eye-to-eye with the sheriff's dark, penetrating gaze. She felt a little intimidated, but refused to back down. "Angie lives a couple of doors away," she said vaguely. "I've got a letter here for her."

"She's one of Chicago Joe's working girls, eh?"

"I've heard that name before. Just who is Chicago Joe?"

Paden's thin, black mustache twitched. "Her name is Josephine Martin and she comes from Chicago, or so the story goes. She enlisted her, uh, talents in the war and kept up the soldiers' spirits. How fortunate we are," he added with sarcasm, "that she decided to settle in Silverstone and take in young women who have nowhere else to go."

"She takes in young women?"

Paden inclined his head slightly. "*Sí,* but in exchange they have to work for her. It's hardly a charitable act. Chicago Joe is making a fortune, and her girls are dirt poor."

"Well, that doesn't seem very fair."

He chuckled. "Life is not fair; haven't you learned that by now?"

She shrugged. "But God is fair. Always."

"Hm. . ."

Bethany's face warmed as she recalled hearing earlier that the sheriff had frequented the disgraceful establishment last night and she couldn't make herself meet his gaze. "Well, I. . . I just want to deliver a letter, that's all. I won't be long."

"And what do you think the good pastors will have to say about your mail service?"

"They don't have to know." Bethany lifted her chin, but she still avoided the sheriff's dark eyes. "They're both out of town."

"I see." Paden lifted his hands. "Well, I think your plan is unwise, but I will not stop you."

"Thank you, Sheriff." Bethany turned on her heel and left his office. After a few short steps, however, she could already see the wisdom in his words. The alley was littered with broken glass and empty liquor bottles. An unkempt man lay to one side, either sleeping or dead, steeped in his own filth. Looking back over her shoulder, she spied Paden Montano at the doorway and was comforted by his presence. She watched as he lit a cheroot, a sure sign that he'd be there a while. Whirling around, she quickly walked the rest of the way to the brothel.

At her knock, the back door opened slowly, cautiously, revealing a woman wearing a stained, red satin robe. Her eyes were puffy and her cheeks slightly swollen. Bethany wondered when she'd last had a good night's rest.

"What do you want?" the woman asked sharply, patting her matted dark brown hair.

"I'd like to speak with Angie Brown, please."

"Angie? What do you want with her?"

"I. . .I have something that belongs to her."

The hard-looking woman held out her hand. "Give it to me. I'll see Angie gets it."

Bethany shook her head. "No. I need to give it to her myself, if you please."

The door slammed in her face. Bethany had nearly given up, when the door opened again and there Angie stood. A frown creased her golden brows.

"What are you doing here?"

Smiling, Bethany held out the letter. "This came for you today in a packet of mail that accidentally got shipped to Fort Yuma. I had a feeling you'd want to see it right away."

"Oh. . .?" Angie took the proffered envelope and then gasped. "It came! She answered my letter!" Angie clutched it to her heart. "There is a God after all."

"Of course there is." Bethany pointed at the letter. "Is it from home?"

"Sort of. I contacted my step-sister in San Francisco, never really expecting a reply. We were never close."

Bethany nodded, hoping Angie would say more.

"But it's important to me just the same. Thank you so much for risking your good name to bring me this letter."

"You're welcome, but I was just trying to be a good Christian woman."

Angie snorted contemptuously. "This town is full of 'good Christian women'—and their good Christian husbands come and visit me after they get paid." Her laughter was bitter. "Hypocrites, that's what Christians are!"

"Some, yes, but not all." Bethany felt insulted, although she was more infuriated with those who had ruined Christ's reputation with their sinful actions. "And the Lord Himself is certainly no hypocrite. He is the same yesterday, today, and forever. Perfect."

Angie lifted a doubtful brow. "Well, maybe He is—and maybe you're different. We'll see."

Bethany smiled at the challenge. "Say, do you like to

read?" As the question rolled off her tongue, she wondered where it came from, and she felt momentarily embarrassed for asking.

However, Angie's reply alleviated her embarrassment. "I love to read. . .but I don't have any books. None of the other girls own many, and what they've got I've read."

"I have a lot of books. They were donated to the school, and many of them aren't fitting for children, but they're fine for adults. I'd be happy to share."

"Would you?" Angie's face glowed.

"I'll gather together a few volumes and bring them by tomorrow. Is that all right?"

"You're comin' back here?"

"I'll try."

"You're crazy." Angie shook her head. "Something tells me you won't be teaching school here come fall—not if you keep company with me."

"No one has to know." Bethany held out her right hand. "Friends?"

"Are you *loco*? You can't be friends with me."

Bethany stood undaunted, her hand outstretched.

Finally, Angie acquiesced. "Friends. . .at your own risk, mind you."

"See you tomorrow." Smiling, Bethany turned and began making her way down the alley. Sheriff Montano was still leaning up against the doorjamb, waiting for her.

"Your good deed for the day?" His dark eyes shone with amusement.

"Something like that. Thank you, Sheriff."

Without so much as a backward glance, Bethany left Paden's office and crossed Main Street. Several passers-by called greetings to her, and she politely acknowledged them. Oddly, the heat didn't seem quite so stifling. She entered the boardinghouse, left word that she'd be at school, then quickly departed to select some books for Angie.

eight

Luke and Jacob returned from Arizona City early the next morning, driving a passenger wagon pulled by a team of mules with their horses tethered behind it. In the plank seat, directly in back of the men, were two lovely women. The one Bethany recognized as Grace Elliot, Jacob's fiancée. The other, she didn't know.

From her second-story bedroom window, she watched the men jump from their perches and then help the ladies down. Even at this distance, Bethany could see that the woman to whom Luke extended his hand was beautiful. Her bright blond hair was neatly tucked into a stiff white bonnet that matched the lacy collar of her yellow dress. Luke's hands were at her waist as she alighted from the wagon, and when her feet touched the street, she looked up at him with such a come-hither expression that it sent a surge of jealousy, hot and bitter, coursing through Bethany's veins. Her chest muscles constricted—or was that her heart breaking?—when she thought she saw Luke looking back.

Bethany was transported back to last summer when Sarah McCabe first came to Milwaukee, capturing Richard Navis's heart. *It's happening again,* she thought. *Dear Lord, please. . . not again.*

Turning, she caught a glimpse of herself in the looking glass and paused for a moment of self-examination. She wore a simple blue and tan plaid cotton dress—hardly a match for that woman's sunny yellow gown. But it was fitting for chores, since she had promised to help Mrs. Baker with the cleaning today. She couldn't very well wear her Sunday best! But look at her hair! Bethany expelled a forlorn sigh. Already several wispy strands had escaped her chignon.

"Oh, so what!" she muttered to her reflection. "So what if Luke changes his mind about marrying me and falls in love with that. . .that gorgeous creature. I'll always be a plain little mouse." Bethany turned and headed toward the door. "Besides, it happened before, it'll happen again. I should be used to it by now!"

She flung the door open with unnecessary force, then gasped with surprise. "Luke!"

He frowned. "Were you talking to someone?"

"Um. . .no. I was just memorizing a passage of Scripture."

"Really?" He looked pleased. "Which one?"

"Oh, ah, I can't remember. I guess I need more practice." Her lie sent a wave of guilt rushing over her.

"It'll come." Leaning against the doorjamb, he smiled in a way that made her feel even worse.

"So, how was your trip?" she asked nervously.

"Fine. I sent off the telegram to your father, although it may be a while till we hear back."

Bethany nodded, worrying her lower lip as a vision of Luke assisting the woman in yellow crossed her mind.

"You still want to get married, don't you?"

"Y–Yes," she hedged. "I guess so."

"You guess so?" Luke's eyes narrowed. "What's wrong, Beth?"

"Nothing. . .everything!" Throwing her hands in the air, she turned and walked back into the room. "Oh, never mind." When Luke didn't reply, she pivoted around and saw his baffled expression. It matched her own confused, insecure feelings. If only she were beautiful and Luke loved her. If only she could work up the nerve to speak her mind!

She watched him now as he scratched the back of his head, still looking puzzled. Then he put his hands on his hips. "I reckon we ought to have a good long talk."

"No, Luke, I'm fine. Really."

"You look unhappy."

"No. . .I'm. . .well, I don't know how to describe it."

Luke's features softened. "I don't guess I proposed in a very romantic way. Catherine even accused me of strong-arming you into accepting. I didn't mean—"

"Who's Catherine?" Bethany interrupted.

He smiled patiently. "Catherine Elliot Harrison is Grace's cousin. The entire Elliot family has been as close as kin to the McCabes for as long as I can remember. Catherine came out west to help Grace with wedding plans." Luke's expression turned solemn. "But she's going through the fire, Beth. She lost her husband, Stephen, in the war about a year and a half ago. She's still hurting badly."

Bethany imagined Luke would offer a wonderful consolation for the poor, dear widow; however, she didn't voice the biting response. And she vehemently wished she didn't feel so hateful.

"I want you to meet her," Luke continued, obviously unaware of the battle raging inside of Bethany. "She's downstairs right now and I've got high hopes of you two becoming fast friends. Oh, and I should add that Mrs. Baker is about to serve breakfast. That's why I came up to fetch you."

As if on cue, Doris Baker's voice sailed up the stairwell. "Pastor Luke? Are you and Bethany coming down soon?"

"Be right there," he called over his shoulder. He turned back to Bethany. "Let's set aside some time to talk, all right?"

"No need. I'm fine, Luke."

ॐ

As everyone lit into their breakfasts with healthy appetites, Luke became increasingly aware of Bethany picking at hers. Moreover, she didn't add a single word to the conversation, but just sat there beside him, looking miserable.

Heavenly Father, he prayed silently, *perhaps I did coerce Beth into agreeing to marry me. But it seems so right. . .the two of us. And the timing couldn't have been better, what with her reputation being in question. Just maybe I went about it all wrong. Can I somehow make amends? Will You help me?*

"And that there package arrived from Prescott for the sheriff," Mr. Baker was saying. Luke only caught the last part his sentence, so it didn't make much sense. "I expected he'd come for breakfast, but he didn't show."

Bethany seemed to perk up. Her eyes went to the long counter in the lobby on which the parcel lay. Then she stood and excused herself, quickly leaving the table and running up the stairs. If Luke felt bewildered by her odd behavior, he was even more perplexed when she reappeared with an armful of books.

"I've got a few errands to run," she announced, suddenly looking as cheerful as a picnic, "so I'll take this package to the sheriff."

"Well, that's mighty considerate of you, but—"

Before Ed even finished his sentence, Bethany had grabbed the package and rushed out the door.

Glancing at the confounded expressions around him, Luke stood, smiling politely to conceal his chagrin. " 'Scuse me, folks."

Following Bethany, he got as far as the edge of the sun-blanched boardwalk when he saw her enter the sheriff's office, and his blood began to boil. So she was carrying on with Montano after all, huh? Just looking for an excuse to see him. . .

Angrier than he'd ever felt, Luke crossed the street. He had a mind to take that girl over his knee. No wonder she looked none-too-pleased to see him this morning. However, his mind had a hard time grasping that reality.

He entered the sheriff's office and found Paden standing at the back door, holding his package in one hand and his gun in the other. "Touch that woman and it's the last thing you will ever do, my friend." His voice was filled with a venomous warning that stopped Luke in his tracks. Then he added, "Make haste, *chiquita,* I have work to do."

"What in the world is going on here?" Luke demanded, the fight draining from him, to be replaced by utter confusion.

The sheriff turned to him, and grinned wryly. "Ah, Pastor, you have returned from Arizona City, I see."

"Sure have." His eyes narrowed. "Where's Beth?"

The sheriff glanced down the alleyway. "She is just now knocking on the brothel's back door."

"What?"

"Seems she has befriended one of the prostitutes." Paden's grin broadened. "But I will let her explain."

"And she will, trust me." Luke sauntered farther into the office. "Mind if I wait here?"

"Be my guest." Gazing back out the door, the sheriff let out an irritable-sounding sigh. "You might want to inform our little schoolteacher that this time of the morning is not so good to use the alley, particularly for a woman. It is filled with riffraff off the docks and drunks sleeping off last night's booze."

"I'll be sure to tell her." *Along with a few other choice words,* he added silently. Settling into the wooden chair in front of the desk, Luke waited for Bethany to return.

෨

"You can't keep coming here," Angie scolded.

"But I brought you some books, just as I promised."

"I know and I appreciate that, but. . .well, it's too danger-ous for you to come here."

"The sheriff's guarding me."

"Yes, I see." Angie glanced down the alley. "But you're still asking for trouble, if not from the despicable characters back here, then from Chicago Joe. She won't like it that we're keeping company."

"Can you and I meet somewhere else?"

Angie shrugged.

"Please," Bethany asked sweetly. "I need a friend and I think maybe you do, too."

Angie laughed. "There are plenty of other women who'll be your friend, little Christian girl. Now, go. . .and leave me alone."

Bethany felt hurt by the rejection. Yet she could hardly force a friendship. "Well, all right." She swallowed hard, willing herself not to cry. But the truth was she did need a friend—another women with whom she could converse, someone she could trust. And there was just something about Angie Brown that tugged at her heart and made her believe that beneath the hard veneer lay a soft, lonely heart in need of companionship. But there wasn't much she could do about it if Angie refused her efforts. "I'll be on my way."

"Want your books back?"

"No, you may keep them."

Bethany turned and began to take her leave when Angie's voice halted her steps.

"Do you know where the western ridge is?"

Turning, Bethany shook her head.

"Well, ask somebody for directions. I go there every morning about sun-up to. . .to clear my head. . .and think."

Smiling, Bethany nodded, then continued on to the sheriff's office. Progress!

"Thank you for the protection, Sheriff." She slipped past him.

"My pleasure."

His husky tone made her bristle, but she went on down the rickety stairs without further comment. Two steps later, she looked up and gasped with horror. "Luke!"

He lifted his blond brows and a hint of irony crossed his features.

"Seems you have some explaining to do, *chiquita,*" Paden said behind her. He sounded thoroughly amused.

She cast him a dubious glance before returning her gaze to Luke's. "I'm not doing anything wrong."

"I'm glad to hear that," Luke replied flatly.

The sheriff chuckled, much to Bethany's aggravation. Then Luke held his hand out to her. She took it at once and he led her across Main Street. Reaching the other side, they walked down the boardwalk, and Bethany had to fairly trot in order to keep up with his long strides. As if sensing her efforts, Luke slowed his pace, although he didn't release her hand. Was he angry? He looked angry.

Bethany kept silent all the way through town and even held her peace after they reached the little road that took them out to the exact spot where he'd suggested they get married. Only then did she speak up.

"Luke, hear me out. Please."

He dropped her hand. "I intend to. Have a seat."

Sitting on a large, flat rock near the bluff, Bethany couldn't tell if he'd stated the remark sarcastically, but she hoped he'd listen.

He sat down beside her. "All right, let's have it."

To the best of her ability, Bethany explained how she'd met Angie Brown in the general store and how she felt burdened for her. She told him how she'd used the excuse of delivering mail yesterday to talk to her and that she devised the plan of running through the sheriff's office as a means to get to the brothel unnoticed.

"But I won't have to do that anymore because Angie said I could meet her at the western ridge. Will you tell me how to get there?"

"Yes," Luke answered calmly, "but let me ask you this: Did you ever consider how it might look to anyone else who watched you enter the sheriff's office and not come out for a good measure of time?"

Bethany inhaled sharply.

"Obviously you didn't."

She expelled a long, slow breath. "Luke, I just don't think that way. I don't have a suspicious mind."

"I know," he replied on a softer note. He took her hand and held it between the both of his. "You're young and tend to believe the best of folks. But trust me, darlin', the world is rude and unkind and many times Christians are, too."

Bethany smiled, mostly because he'd called her "darlin'." He'd never done that before and it made her feel special.

"Now, I aim to ask you one more thing," he said with a serious expression, "and I want you to give me an honest reply."

"All right."

Luke paused, looking momentarily pensive. "Do you have feelings for Paden Montano?"

"What kind of feelings? I mean, I do find him rather irksome. I suppose that's a feeling, although I did appreciate his protection while I visited Angie."

"Beth, I'm supposed to do the protecting, not him. And I guess it bothers me that you didn't give me a yes or no answer." He searched her face and Bethany felt her face warming to a blush from the intensity of his gaze. "Let me rephrase the question. Are you in love with the sheriff?"

"No!"

"Good."

Wide-eyed, Bethany pulled her hand from Luke's. "How can you even ask me such a thing?"

"Because I'm a jealous fool, Beth, that's how."

A surprised laugh made its way from her throat, nearly choking her. "At least you're an honest one." She smiled broadly.

Luke smiled, too.

Bethany stood, picked up a stone, and tossed it aimlessly over the cliff. She pondered the idea of asking Luke who he was in love with, but somehow the words wouldn't form in her throat. However, another confession did take shape in her mind.

"Luke, I have to be truthful about something." She turned and faced him.

"Oh?"

"Yes. I lied to you this morning. I wasn't memorizing Scripture in my room. I was complaining aloud and when you overheard, I was too ashamed to admit it."

"Hm. . .well, I forgive you, Beth, and if you ask the Lord to do the same, He will."

She nodded, lowering her chin and gazing at the rocky terrain beneath her feet. "Concerning the Lord, Luke, I think you should know that I am not a very spiritual person. That is, I have trouble reading my Bible. Other books come alive in my mind, but not God's Word." She looked up at him. "Some pastor's wife I'll make."

Luke's blue eyes regarded her intently. "Is that what's been bothering you?"

Bethany shrugged, unable to divulge that she, too, felt like a "jealous fool" after watching Catherine Harrison's arrival.

"Listen, you get that silly notion right out of your head," Luke told her. "You're going to make me a fine wife. I've prayed about us, Beth, and I truly believe you're the one God has chosen for me. Why, I have every confidence you'll help move my ministry forward. You're a hard worker, kind, sweet-spirited, patient. . ."

"I'm not patient with Millie Baker. The girl makes me crazy!"

Luke grinned. "But you don't let it show. Some folks get right sore with her. And as for having trouble reading your Bible, I'll help you, Beth. We'll tackle it together. All right?"

"All right."

Luke stood to his feet. "We'll be happy, I promise," he said with a smile that reached his eyes.

Bethany met his gaze. "You're sure? You really want to marry me?"

"I'm positive."

He offered his arm, she took it, and they ambled back to town looking every bit the adoring couple. But all the while, Bethany longed to ask him the foremost question on her mind—the one that she couldn't seem to force past her lips. *What about love, Luke McCabe? What about love?* Her heart sank. She might as well be marrying Ralph Ames!

nine

Bethany wanted to hate Catherine Harrison. The woman was as beautiful as Bethany was plain. Her eyes were robin's egg blue and her delicate, creamy-white skin was unmarred by tan and freckles, causing Bethany to wish she'd worn her bonnet more often. Catherine's sunny-blond hair was thick, naturally wavy, and it obediently stayed pinned, whereas Bethany's own sparrow-brown strands were as straight as nails and refused to remain in any sort of neat coil. However, Catherine seemed kind and good-natured and against her will, Bethany found herself liking the woman.

"She reminds me of your sister, Sarah," Bethany remarked as she and Luke strolled to the western ridge the next morning. He had insisted upon escorting her out of town but promised to "stay out of the way" so she and Angie could visit.

"I reckon she does resemble Sarah," Luke agreed, "but Catherine is a refined version, wouldn't you say?"

"Refined? Yes, Catherine is that, all right."

Bethany fretted over her lower lip, wondering if Luke preferred "refined" to her less-than-sophisticated demeanor. She'd grown up on a farm with rough-and-tumble brothers. She could do chores like a boy; her father had often said so. And it was for that very reason she and Sarah had become dear friends by the end of last summer. Sarah was, in Luke's own words, "a high-spirited little minx," and Bethany worried that, perhaps, she fell into the same category.

But maybe she could change. If she set her mind to it, she could learn to be just like Catherine, elegantly poised, speaking in a soft sing-song voice.

Just as the idea took form, Bethany tripped over a small rock in the road and would have fallen head-long into the gravel if Luke hadn't grabbed her upper arm.

"Careful there, Beth."

Her face flamed with embarrassment. So much for grace and polish!

He chuckled, but didn't release her arm. No doubt he had every confidence she'd trip again.

"Remember that time on the trail when Don Thorton fell over a big ol' tree root in the mountains? We all thought he was going to sail right over the ledge, but praise God he didn't. When we all got through holding our breath, we laughed till our sides ached and poor Thorton felt so embarrassed, he wished he would have fallen over the side of the mountain."

Bethany grinned. She remembered.

"You know," Luke stated thoughtfully now, "there's something about traveling with people that makes a body grow closer to them. Like you, Beth, I feel like I've known you half my life. I reckon that's why I sprung a marriage proposal on you like I did." He shrugged, looking sheepish. "Then, again, Jacob is fond of saying I'm as impetuous as the apostle Peter."

Her smile broadened. "I rather agree with Pastor Jake."

Luke gave her a good jostling in payment for the glib remark.

"Stop, Luke, you're going to shake my brains loose!" But Bethany's protest got lost somewhere between their laughter.

Suddenly the ridge came into view and they ceased their horseplay.

"That must be Angie, huh?" Luke nodded toward the lone figure standing in the shadows of the early morning.

"It is. Shall I introduce you?"

He nodded. "And afterwards, I'll make myself scarce." His eyes still twinkled from their merriment, yet he looked at her so hard she blushed. Bethany lowered her gaze, deciding instead to concentrate on her gait.

Nearer to Angie, Bethany called out a greeting. The young woman faced them, casting a suspicious glance at Luke.

"This is Miss Angie Brown," Bethany began. "Angie, please meet my. . .um. . .pastor. . .Pastor Luke McCabe."

"You can say it, Beth," he teased. "I'm your intended." Looking at Angie, he said, "We're only recently betrothed, so she forgets sometimes."

He gave her an affectionate nudge with his elbow, and Bethany smiled. But Angie just nodded curtly.

"Well, I'll be moving along," Luke announced, clearing his throat. "Nice to meet your acquaintance, ma'am." Turning to Bethany, he winked charmingly, then strode off along the stony trail.

"The weather is cool this morning," Bethany stated, making herself comfortable on one of the rock formations.

"Usually is this time of day."

"I prefer this to the dreadful heat." She sighed. "I wonder if I'll ever get accustomed to Arizona."

Angie considered her momentarily. "Where are you from?"

"Wisconsin."

"Mm. . ."

"How 'bout you?"

"Virginia."

"How did you get here? To Silverstone?"

"My step-father. He met my mother on business out east, married her, and moved us all to San Francisco." Angie turned and sat down across from Bethany. "He was a gambler and gold digger. Never did strike it rich, but he traipsed all over the region testing his luck. Found he didn't have any. So he turned to drinking and my mother fretted herself right into the grave. Then one night he came home full of booze and forced himself on me."

"Oh, Angie!" Bethany closed her eyes in horror. "I'm so sorry!"

Angie gave an indignant toss of her head. "He made me what I am today and I curse his name with every breath I take." Raising a taunting brow, she added, "Still wanna be friends?"

Bethany met the challenge with a hearty, "Yes."

An awkward silence grew between them, and Bethany felt a lump of pity and anger forming in her throat. She couldn't fathom a step-father committing such an evil act. "I would have killed the man, had he done that to me!" she declared vehemently. At Angie's shocked expression, she quickly retracted her statement. "Oh, forgive me, please. That wasn't a very Christian-like remark, was it?"

Angie shrugged. "I wouldn't know." She eyed Bethany speculatively. "You think you would have killed him? Really?"

"I'm not sure," Bethany hedged, thinking it over. She remembered how sad she felt after hearing about the ambush, in spite of the fact that those men had been bent on murdering the Indians. "My mother always told me I act before I think. I suppose I just spoke before I thought, because I abhor violence. Maybe I would have wanted to kill him, but I doubt I'd really do it."

"Well, I dreamed about killing my step-father," Angie admitted, staring out into the vast shrouds of jagged ridges. "Wished I would have, but instead I ran away. Came here." Her voice crumbled. "And now I'd rather be dead."

"Shh, you mustn't say that." Bethany moved to sit beside the young woman whose blue eyes looked vacant. Bethany looped a compassionate arm around her slender shoulders.

"Sometimes I come here and think about throwing myself off the ledge over there. But I'm too scared."

"And you should be. Eternity awaits." Bethany struggled with her next words, praying inwardly. "Would you be ready, Angie?" she asked at last. "To meet God Almighty?"

Turning, Angie gazed into Bethany's face. "Meet God? No. I won't meet Him. My soul will plunge straight to Hell when I die."

"Doesn't have to, Angie."

Her eyes narrowed distrustfully. "Don't you understand what I am?"

"Yes, but Mary Magdalene was a. . .well, she had the same profession."

"Who's that?" Angie asked cynically. "Mary. . .who?"

"Mary Magdalene. She lived a sinful life. But then she met Jesus of Nazareth, the Messiah. He's God's only begotten Son and was sent from Heaven nearly two thousand years ago, clothed in humanity, to save those who'll repent of their sins and believe in Him." She paused. "Mary Magdalene was saved and you can be, too!"

Angie sat there with a stunned expression. "Where'd you hear that?"

"It's in the Bible, and. . .well, Luke preaches it all the time."

"The Bible?" Her eyes widened slightly. "It mentions working girls getting. . .saved? From Hell?"

Bethany nodded. "Would you like to read it for yourself? You can borrow mine."

The nod was ever so slight, but visible enough to encourage Bethany. "I'll bring it tomorrow morning."

Angie stood and tipped her head with a sudden aloofness. "I must be going. If Chicago Joe wakes up and I'm not there I'll really wish I were dead."

Bethany rose from the boulder. "Is she truly from Chicago? That's not far from Wisconsin."

"What?" Angie regarded her as though she'd sprouted antlers. Then she shook her head in wonder. "You know what you are? You're like sugar. You make even a bitter pill taste sweet. 'Not far from Wisconsin,'" she mimicked in falsetto before chuckling. "Looks like you and Chicago Joe have something in common, eh? Lake Michigan!"

Bethany forced a smile, not quite sure if she'd been insulted. "Well," she finally said, giving a careless shrug, "I'm certainly impressed by your geographical knowledge."

Angie's mirth escalated until she had to sit back down. She laughed and laughed and tears streamed from her eyes. "Oh, Sugar," she said breathlessly, "I haven't laughed like that in a hundred years."

Bethany rolled her eyes. "Really, Angie, you can't be more than twenty-five."

"Nineteen," she corrected, the last of her humor dying. "But I feel like I'm ninety-nine!"

≈

"Sounds like you had a right good talk with Angie," Luke remarked after he listened to Bethany relay their entire conversation.

"I told her I'd come back tomorrow."

"Fine by me. I'll fetch you at the boardinghouse nice and early. It's not safe for you to come out here alone, so wait for me. Understand?"

"Yes, I just wish Angie would have allowed us to walk her back home."

"I know, darlin'. But don't go getting it into your head that you can venture out by yourself like she does. Honest, Beth. It's not safe."

"I won't. I promise. I'll wait for you tomorrow morning. Just don't be late!"

He brought his chin back and his eyes sparkled mischievously. "Bossy little thing, aren't you?"

She laughed softly in reply and stepped closer to him, tucking her hand into the crook of his arm. He covered it with his own warm and callused one, and for a moment Bethany could almost pretend they were really in love.

When they got back to town, Luke set out to meet with the grieving families of the men killed in the ambush while Bethany assisted Mrs. Baker with the washing. She hung clean clothes and linens on the line with Millie's help on her right and Catherine's on her left. They chattered over her head like two twittering birds in the treetops until Bethany hushed them.

"If you continue your prattling, the Indians will hear and they'll attack the whole town."

Catherine gasped.

"Oh, go on with you, Miss Stafford," Millie said disbelievingly. But she glanced warily toward the outer ridges and fairly whispered the rest of the afternoon.

Later that evening, the boardinghouse dining room filled to capacity as the stage rolled in, depositing hungry and weary travelers. Bethany helped Mrs. Baker serve, as it was all Rosalinda could do to keep up with the cooking. Millie whined when her mother asked for her assistance, and soon Mrs. Baker simply gave up trying to coax her into the kitchen. So Bethany tried to persuade the girl.

"Come along, Millie. We need you."

"But I'm tired from all the washing and hanging."

"Me, too. But there's still work to be done. Come on. When we do things we don't like, and we wear a smile while doing them, it builds character."

"Character shmaracter. Mrs. Harrison and Miss Elliot don't have to help."

Bethany glanced at Catherine who was talking with Luke, Jacob, and Grace. Bethany squelched the jealous bile rising in her throat. "Mrs. Harrison and Miss Elliot are visitors," she said to Millie more sternly than she'd intended. "Now, come along."

Much to her amazement, the girl acquiesced. "You're a fright when you're angry, Miss Stafford!" Millie pouted. "It's like little sparks fly from your eyes."

"Nonsense." Bethany chanced a final glance at Luke. However, she relished the thought of sending a few sparks in his direction, as he seemed to be enjoying Catherine's company far more than propriety dictated.

☙

At last Bethany finished up with her share of the kitchen duty. She unfastened the apron with tired arms and hung it up before making her way back through the now-empty dining room. She'd all but assumed everyone had retired for the night, when she heard voices out in front of the boarding-house. Then a female's delicate laughter reached her ears, followed by a man's hearty chuckle.

"Oh, Luke, you are so droll." Catherine's honeyed voice wafted through the opened front door.

Bethany stood in the shadows, knowing she ought not listen yet unable to budge.

"I reckon I'll take that as a compliment," she heard him reply.

"It is a compliment. . .oh, Luke," she cooed, "it's so good to see you again. I'll cherish every moment we spent together tonight."

There was an interminable moment of silence, during which Bethany peaked out the doorway. Much to her dismay she saw Catherine gazing up longingly into Luke's face. Obviously, she wanted Luke to kiss her, and for a moment Bethany feared he might. They stood as close as lovers, and when Catherine's light-colored gown caught the breeze, it swirled around Luke's booted ankles.

"Luke," Catherine asked softly, "are you thinking what I'm thinking?"

Bethany's wounded heart wouldn't allow her to stay and hear his reply. With tears threatening to spill, she turned away and ran up the stairs to her room.

ten

"Darlin', as much as you deny it, I know something's wrong. You've barely said two words to me in the past few days!"

The bumpy road leading to Ralph Ames' place threatened to uproot Bethany from the wagon seat, but she held on tightly. . .and said nothing. She feared opening her mouth and spitting nails instead of speaking in complete sentences.

"Did I offend you?" Luke asked for the umpteenth time.

"No," she replied curtly, staring across the desert plain, carefully averting her gaze. She'd never been a good liar. Papa could always tell when she told a fib. He'd look right into her eyes and he'd know. Her concern was that Luke would, too.

"Well, I'm sure glad to hear I didn't offend you," he stated on a note of sarcasm, "because if I had, you'd have a biblical obligation to tell me so. Shunning ain't biblical."

He'd leaned over and drawled the latter so close to her ear that she swatted at him like a pesky fly. He chuckled when she missed. "Beth, I don't know what's gotten into you, but I sure hope you get over it quick-like, or I'm liable to—"

"What?" she snapped. "What will you do? Break our betrothal? Fine. Do it now and get it over with."

Determined to protect the remains of her broken heart, she pretended not to notice the startled look that crossed his tanned face. But much to her dismay, Luke slowed the wagon to a halt in the middle of the seldom-traveled road. The morning sun beat down on them and the air was still and hot against Bethany's already flushed cheeks. Her sunbonnet had proved little use today and more of a nuisance. Not a soul could be seen for miles across this desolate stretch of land, although she knew the Ames' ranch was just over the next hill. But, for now, she and Luke were the only people in sight.

"Mind explaining that last statement?" he asked dryly.

She stubbornly refused, folding her arms in front of her.

"Look, Beth, I'm trying to be patient, but that's not one of my virtues, in case you haven't noticed." He combed frustrated fingers through his thick sandy-blond hair. "Now will you stop playing games and talk to me!"

"Playing games!" Furious, she stood, fists clenched at her side, and it was all she could do to keep from raising her voice. "You want me to talk to you? All right, I'll talk to you." Irritably, she flipped her bonnet backward, allowing it to dangle around her neck. "I don't appreciate the way you and Catherine were keeping company a few nights ago. I saw the way you gazed into her eyes."

"What?" Luke rose slowly, looking perplexed. "I never did any such thing!"

"Oh, you sure did! I saw it! And, worse, I overheard the two of you outside the boardinghouse that same night. It was quite the intimate conversation, if I do say so myself."

"Beth, I don't know what you saw or heard, but you're wrong."

"Really? Then what did she mean by, 'I'll cherish every moment we spent together tonight,' " Bethany drawled, imitating Catherine's velveteen, southern accent. " 'Oh, Luke, are you thinking what I'm thinking?' " She narrowed her gaze. "Stop smiling, it's not funny!"

"You're right, it's not." He wiped the smirk off his face with the back of his hand.

"And for your information, Luke McCabe, forever is a long time to spend with someone on account of a reputation. Therefore. . ." She took a deep, steadying breath. "Therefore, I'm breaking our betrothal so you can marry the one you. . . you really love!"

"Well, that's mighty considerate of you," he retorted, watching her closely. "But just who is this 'one' you're referring to?"

"Catherine, of course. And I hope you two are very happy!"

While the last of her words wished him well, Bethany's heart cursed him to the depths of the earth. But in the next moment, she felt ashamed for her ungodly behavior. Her anger waned. "Catherine will make a much better pastor's wife than I," she stated, doing her best to avoid his probing gaze. "She's sweet, good, and kind, and I'm not. . .as you can see. We're ill-suited, Luke."

"Ill-suited, huh?"

She replied with a shrug, feeling her chin quiver slightly before sitting down hard on the wagon seat. Enough said; she wished he'd get on to the Ames'. She had a long day ahead of her, caring for children, washing, ironing, fixing meals.

Silently, Luke took his place on the bench, slapped the reins, and within moments the horses resumed their steady trot. A heavy silence hung between them until finally Ralph's property came into view.

"You've got a fiery temperament for a young woman, I'll grant you that," Luke remarked, driving the wagon past the cabin, and bringing it to a stop near the stable. He wound the reins around the break handle. "But I think you're every bit as sweet, good, and kind as Catherine. And, just for the record, I'm not in love with her. Furthermore, I would suggest the next time you listen in on someone else's conversation you wait it out and hear the whole thing."

Bethany chafed beneath the reprimand. "I didn't intend on hearing any of it."

"Well, fine. But the fact is, you did, and you missed a crucial part. You didn't hear what I said, except I might just be mad enough right now not to want to tell you."

Bethany sighed unhappily as Luke jumped from his perch. She felt bad for angering him, yet relieved to have aired her insecurities. She was even encouraged to hear Luke didn't love Catherine. *But does he love me?* she wondered. *Will he ever?*

Warily she watched as he raised his hands to assist her descent. But when her feet touched the gravel driveway, his arms encircled her waist, pulling her against him, holding her tightly.

"Luke, I don't think—"

His mouth came down on hers, cutting off further protests. She struggled against him, trying to push him away, but slowly she decided she rather enjoyed the feeling of his lips tenderly caressing her own. As if sensing her surrender, Luke deepened the kiss, sending delicious shivers down her spine.

Then all too soon, it was over.

Luke smiled down into her eyes as the dreamy haze lifted from her vision. "Darlin'," he murmured, brushing his lips against hers one last time, "I don't think we're ill-suited at all."

"Oh, you!" Feeling more embarrassed than exasperated, Bethany pushed against his chest. "Some pastor you turned out to be!"

He released her, chuckling. "First and foremost I'm a man, Beth, and you were a woman in need of a good kissing."

"Hmpf!" Bethany stomped off toward the cabin, but stopped in mid-stride. Turning, she faced him once more. He still wore a rakishly handsome grin as he began unhitching the team.

"May I ask you something, please?"

"Certainly."

Bethany closed the distance between them and whispered, "Did you ever kiss Catherine like you just kissed me?"

"I never kissed Catherine ever. Does that make you feel better?"

"Yes, actually, it does," she returned, lifting her chin primly and wishing he didn't look quite so amused.

Spinning on her heel, she recommenced her stroll to the Ames' cabin, listening to Luke's laughter sailing off behind her on the sweltering breeze.

❧

The oldest of Ralph Ames' eight children, Regina—or "Reggie" as she preferred—was twelve; Jesse, age eleven; Ethan had just turned ten; Eunice was nine; Mary Elizabeth, eight; Jeb, five; Lorena, four; and baby Michael, whom the Cantons had cared for up until two days ago, was almost two months old.

"There would have been more of us kids," Regina had once informed Bethany, "but Mama lost two babies in between Mary Elizabeth and Jeb, and two more between Lorena and Michael."

Regina, Bethany had long since noticed, was the little mother figure now that her mama was dead, and the young girl bore a great responsibility on her slender shoulders. Today she looked worn and peaked, holding baby Michael who was screaming at the top of his lungs.

"He won't stop, Miss Stafford," she said, looking as though she might burst into tears herself. "I haven't slept all night."

"When did he last feed?" Bethany asked, removing her bonnet and placing it over a wooden chair.

"Well, that's just it. He won't feed at all. And Pa. . .he's been hollerin' an awful lot because the baby won't quit cryin'. But he's cryin' on account of Pa's hollerin'!"

"Where's your father now?" Bethany took the wailing baby out of Reggie's arms. She hadn't seen this child yet, since he'd lived all his eight weeks at the Cantons' place.

The girl sighed with relief, her burden lifted. "Pa's in the stable."

"In the stable?" Bethany felt herself flush.

"Yes, ma'am."

She turned from the girl and bounced the baby in her arms, praying Ralph Ames hadn't observed her and Luke just minutes ago.

"Oh, Miss Stafford," Reggie cried in a rare display of emotion, "I'm so glad you've come!" She threw her arms around Bethany's waist and laid her head on her shoulder. "Everything's been just awful since Mama's passing."

"There, there," Bethany replied above the din of Michael's bawling, "it will all work out. You'll see."

It took Bethany nearly an hour to calm the baby, but finally he fell into a sound sleep. She hushed the other children each time they came bursting into the one-room home.

"Why do we gotta use quiet voices?" Lorena asked, doing her best to whisper. She was an adorable child with strawberry blond curls.

"Baby Michael's sleeping," Bethany replied, cutting up a freshly plucked chicken for supper.

"Oh."

"Shh!" Ethan commanded his little sister.

In reply, she stuck her tongue out at him, then buried her face in Bethany's skirt.

"Would you like to help me, sweetie?" she asked the little girl.

Lorena shook her head and clung to Bethany, sucking her thumb. *She needs a mama,* Bethany mused. *Someone to rock her and read to her. . .*

Bethany recalled Ralph's proposal. As much as she would enjoy mothering his children, she certainly didn't relish the idea of becoming his wife. She thought of Luke's kiss. . . she'd never been kissed like that before and she shuddered as she imagined Ralph in a husbandly role. She was only too glad that Luke had promised to stay around all day, so Ralph wouldn't try to coerce her into marrying him again.

"Pa sure looks mad," Jesse said, staring outside. None of the windows had panes of glass, just wooden shutters that could be closed against the hot sunshine or cold rain. "And just listen to him layin' into Pastor Luke!"

"What's he sayin'?" Mary Elizabeth asked.

"I can't quite hear."

With Lorena still clutching her skirts, Bethany stepped to the window and looked out. Ralph seemed to be shouting about something, all right, and Luke was the recipient. "Come away from here and help me peel the potatoes, please."

Jesse groaned, but obeyed.

"Do you think they'll have a fist fight?" Ethan wanted to know.

"Of course not!" Bethany sounded more confident than she felt. She felt sure Luke wouldn't throw any punches, but she didn't trust Ralph. However, for the children's sakes, she added, "Christian men don't have to use their fists to solve problems. They have God!"

"Yeah, you lead-head."

"Jesse, I'll have none of that talk. Now apologize to your brother at once."

"Pa calls me and Ethan 'lead-head' all the time. Ain't a bad thing if Pa does it."

Bethany nibbled her lower lip. Hollering and name-calling from the man of the house? How atrocious! Something had to be done. . .but what?

Within a relatively short time, Bethany had dinner ready and everyone gathered around the table. Ralph prayed over the food, but his heart wasn't in it. He looked mean and angry as he gulped down his food. Clearly, he hadn't shaved in weeks, and both his scraggy beard and his hair were filthy. His clothes were sweat-stained, and Bethany got the distinct impression he didn't like to change his shirt and pants often.

Luke, on the other hand, seemed his lighthearted self, obviously unaffected by whatever Ralph had been shouting at him about earlier.

"Beth, this is a mighty tasty meal."

"Thank you, Luke." She felt pleased by the compliment, yet oddly timid as well. She looked down at Michael, who now lay contentedly in her arms, suckling a bottle of milk.

"I hope you plan on eating," Luke added.

"I will. . .when I'm done feeding the baby."

Smiling, he turned to all the children. "Did you know Miss Stafford once made the most interesting baking-powder biscuits I ever saw?"

"Don't you dare tell them that story!"

"Oh, yes, please! Tell us!" Eunice begged.

"We—we like thtories," five-year-old Jeb stuttered.

Ralph threw his fork down onto his now-empty plate and slid back the chair. The children cowered, while Bethany and Luke exchanged a troubled glance.

"Now, Ralph, aren't you going to stay and listen to this funny tale? I believe it'll even have you smiling."

"No, Preacher, I don't want to hear nothing you have to say." With that, he left the cabin, slamming the door behind him.

Baby Michael began to cry.

"There, there, sweetheart," Bethany crooned until he hushed.

One by one the other children relaxed.

"Tell us the funny story, Pastor Luke," Reggie insisted.

He looked at Bethany and she nodded her consent.

"All right." He grinned. "Well, in order to get here, to Arizona, we joined up with a big wagon train that started off way back in Missouri and while Miss Stafford and I were traveling, she and a nice German lady named Mrs. Schlyterhaus shared the cooking responsibilities.

"So one evening," he said, his eyes twinkling, "I had my mouth all set for some good ol' hot biscuits. . .you know, the kind that melt in your mouth?"

Already the children were smiling.

"But what do you suppose happens when I bite into one of Miss Stafford's creations?"

"What?" they cried.

"It don't let go!" Luke replied dramatically. "My biscuit stretched like gum, longer and longer, then it snapped right back in my face."

Reggie put her hand over her mouth and giggled.

"Did you finally eat it?" Ethan asked.

"No, sir. It didn't want to get ate. But it wasn't long till I discovered those biscuits had some bounce and pretty soon me and some other boys were tossing them at each other."

"A ball game? With biscuits?" Jesse laughed and the other

children hooted, adding their own silly remarks.

"Well, here's the best part. I got friendly with those boys and told them about Jesus. Three of them got saved that very night!"

"Did you hear the angels rejoicing in heaven?" Mary Elizabeth asked.

"You know, I believe I did. What about you, Miss Stafford?" Luke turned toward Bethany. "Did you hear the angels after the boys got saved?"

She shook her head. "All I heard was Mrs. Schlyterhaus muttering about my ruining a batch of perfectly good biscuits. I never did figure out what happened."

"I know!" Jesse said. "The angels got into your recipe when you weren't looking so Pastor Luke could have a ball game and tell those boys Jesus died for their sins."

"Quite likely," Luke agreed. "One never knows how God might use His angels."

The baby had fallen asleep, so Bethany carefully put him into his cradle. Then she dished up a plate of food for herself and ate while the table conversation continued.

Once supper ended, Bethany cleared the dishes, enlisting the girls' help with the washing. Luke lifted little Jeb onto his shoulders as he and Ethan and Jesse ambled outside to find some work.

"I like Pastor Luke," Mary Elizabeth said later as they began gathering soiled laundry.

"Yes, I like him quite well myself." Bethany smiled inwardly. Then, with the girls in tow, Lorena attached to Bethany's skirt, they marched into the yard with the dirty clothes, scrubbed them thoroughly in the wash tub, and hung them out to dry. As the last of it was fastened to the line, baby Michael's cries sounded from inside the cabin.

"Good timing, girls."

Turning, Bethany took several steps toward the house but halted when she saw a figure standing in the shadows under a tree. Seeing the man's coppery skin and long black hair, she inhaled sharply. In one of the Indian's hands, a blade glinted against a slim ray of sunshine streaming through the treetop.

"Luke!" Bethany screamed, shoving the girls behind her. "Luke, come quick!"

Reggie was suddenly beside her. "Are you afraid of Indians, Miss Stafford?"

"Not all. . .only the ones wielding knives. Now get back behind me!" Bethany kept a cautious eye on the brave.

"Oh, you don't have to be afraid of him," Reggie said casually. "That's Warring Spirit. He comes around here all the time."

eleven

Luke came running from the stable with Ralph trailing behind him, rifle in hand. The Indian lifted his knife, but when he saw Ralph, he lowered it.

"Aw, it's just you, Warring Spirit," Ralph muttered.

Luke grinned. "Warring Spirit?"

A flash of recognition entered the brave's dark eyes. "Preacherlukemccabe." He nodded, albeit warily.

"You know him, Luke?" Bethany asked.

"Sort of. We met last week over at Harlan's place."

"Oh, yes. . .I remember you telling me about it."

Ralph began speaking with the Indian in a language Bethany had never heard before, and what he couldn't communicate in the brave's native tongue, he signed with gestures. At last, the Indian chuckled.

"What did you tell him?" Luke wanted to know.

"I done told him to quit scaring the church women who come out here to tend chores. Warring Spirit thinks it's funny."

Bethany clucked her tongue in annoyance as Michael's cries grew more demanding. "The baby. . ."

"Go on, take care of him." Ralph told her, disarming the gun.

She glanced at Luke and he nodded approvingly. Only then did she feel safe to proceed to the cabin.

"Your woman, Preacherlukemccabe?"

Glancing over her shoulder, Bethany saw the Indian point at her.

"Yes, she is my woman," Luke replied without missing a beat.

Her face flamed at the public declaration, but in her heart of hearts, she rejoiced. Luke's woman. Luke's woman! And he meant *her*!

Inside the cabin, she lifted baby Michael into her arms. His face was red and blotchy from weeping. Walking back to the doorway, Bethany called for Reggie to fetch some milk.

"There, there, now," she cooed to the infant, "you'll get fed. I promise."

Gently jostling Michael in the crook of her arm, Bethany stood near the doorway and watched the men talk. She noticed Luke's intent expression and wondered what he was thinking. Knowing him, she guessed he was most likely trying to figure out how to schedule a revival meeting at the Indian's village. Luke seldom missed an opportunity to share Christ.

Reggie returned with a pail of milk. "Can I go back out? I like it when Warring Spirit comes. He sometimes brings us toys. Once he gave Jesse a whistle and he showed me how to make a piece of jewelry."

"That's fine. You go enjoy some free time." Bethany filled a glass baby's bottle. "Might be your last chance for a while since we should start supper soon and after that you're the woman of the house again."

Reggie's smile waned. "Thank you, Miss Stafford."

Poor girl, Bethany mused, *she's as much of a child as the rest, yet she has so much responsibility to bear. . .*

Infant and bottle in hand, she situated herself comfortably in a rocking chair and began feeding Michael. Around them, the cozy home was quiet except for the occasional sound of children's excited voices wafting in from outdoors, and Bethany allowed herself to enjoy the feel of a baby in her arms. Soon, however, she started missing her siblings. Her youngest brother Ned was only four and not too long ago Bethany had snuggled him in her arms. As the oldest of six children, she'd mothered them all, with the exception of the two brothers who were close to her own age. They had been rough-and-tumble playmates, but the little ones were more like real-life baby dolls on whom Bethany practiced her parenting skills.

Her thoughts drifted to her own future children—Luke's

children. The idea was not at all unpleasant. As she rocked Michael, Bethany prayed the Lord would bless her with many babies. *Perhaps if I give Luke plenty of children. . .*

Once more, she recalled the kiss they shared earlier today. Maybe Luke did love her in some small way. The very notion seemed impossible, though.

Why me? The question whirled in her mind. Luke could marry any woman he pleased. In fact, she would have expected he would marry someone like Catherine Harrison, someone beautiful and refined. Yet he'd chosen her, plain Bethany Stafford. Of course, he'd suggested marriage as a remedy for her somewhat blemished reputation—but Luke had made his romantic intentions clear even before that mis-adventure with Sheriff Montano occurred.

But again, why? What on earth attracted him to her? Couldn't he see she was nothing special?

Bethany abandoned solving such a mystery as the work-ings of a man's mind as she gazed at Michael, sleeping angelically for the moment. Standing, she carefully made her way toward the baby's cradle. At that moment, Ralph burst into the cabin with as much tact as a freight train and she silenced him with a wide-eyed look of warning.

"Sorry," he said in hushed tones. "I know women get waspish when us men wake the babies. I'll keep quiet."

"You're very wise, Mr. Ames," Bethany retorted in a whis-per. Turning back to Michael, now wide awake, she grum-bled, "Only you're too late."

"Huh? Oh. . .I apologize."

He peered over her shoulder and considered his son. Turning slightly, Bethany watched him, wondering if Ralph blamed the infant for his wife's death. Or perhaps he blamed himself. Regardless, the bland expression on the man's face masked whatever he felt inside.

"He's got blue eyes," he finally muttered.

"Excuse me?"

"That boy. . .he's the only one of my brood that's got blue

eyes. Rest of thems got brown eyes like me."

Bethany looked down at the baby in her arms. His eyes were definitely blue. Back to Ralph, she asked, "Were your wife's eyes this color?"

"Must've been."

"You mean you're not sure?"

"Aw, now, Miss Stafford, don't use that sharp tone on me. It's been a long time since I stared into a woman's eyes— even if she was my wife. A man gets busy, you know?"

Bethany swallowed a retort, appalled. If he'd taken the time to marry his wife and beget children, he ought to at least know what color their mama's eyes were!

Returning her attention to the baby, she smiled at him lovingly. He gurgled softly as if trying to communicate, and then the most amazing thing happened. Michael's gaze seemed to penetrate her own. She'd never had an infant look at her quite so intensely; in response, something stirred deeply within Bethany's soul. She felt as if her spirit reached out and touched the child's as only a mother's can.

This is my baby.

She shook off the notion as it took form. Of course Michael was not hers—he belonged to Ralph Ames. Yet, an inner prompting, subtle and undefined, seemed to tell her the contrary.

My baby. My baby.

No, he's not!

"That boy sure is fond of you," Ralph observed. He stood close to her ear and his warm breath made her shudder. "Fact is, my children like you best out of all the other church women who come." He lowered his voice and added, "So do I."

Unnerved, Bethany quickly placed Michael in his cradle. "I need to start supper," she said hastily, "or I'll never get home tonight."

❧

Several hours later, Bethany felt more than glad when Luke

assisted her into the wagon and drove off the Ames' property. Almost immediately, she recounted her experience with Michael.

"I've never had anything happen to me quite like it," she told Luke who listened quietly beside her. "It seemed like a premonition, a whisper from Heaven, telling me Michael is going to be my baby and I will be his mother. But if that's true, then God must want me to. . .to marry Mr. Ames. Except. . .oh, Luke! I don't want to!"

"Well, I don't want you to either!" He shook his head as the evening sun sank in the western sky. Hues of pink, violet, red, and orange were painted across the horizon. "Beth, we prayed about this and we both felt it wasn't God's will for you to marry Ralph."

"I know, but now I'm confused."

"More likely you're just tired. You've worked hard today—"

"You're saying my mind is playing tricks on me?" she asked softly, wondering if it were true.

"I'm saying don't rush headlong into any decisions based on some kind of feeling you got while holding a baby."

"But it seemed so real, Luke."

"I'm sure it did."

Bethany chewed her lower lip in consternation. "Have you ever experienced anything similar to what I described?"

"All the time."

She brightened. "Really?"

"Uh-huh. God's Holy Spirit prompts every Christian, but we've got to make sure we're not adding human ideas to the Lord's direction for our lives."

"And you think I am?"

"Well, darlin'," Luke drawled with a smile in his voice, "I've got a mother, two sisters, and a sister-in-law—and it's been my experience that women plus babies equals a whole lot of emotion."

Bethany grinned and inwardly admitted there was a good amount of truth to that statement.

"And don't forget," Luke added, "God is not the author of confusion, but of peace."

"That's in the Bible, isn't it?" she asked, feeling embarrassed she didn't know for sure.

"Sure is. First Corinthians fourteen, verse thirty-three."

Bethany felt her cheeks blush profusely. "I'd have known it myself if I read my Bible more."

"Just how do you go about reading your Bible?"

She shrugged. "I just open it and start reading."

"Anywhere?"

"No, I start at the beginning of a book and read straight through—well, at least I attempt to read straight through. Unfortunately, I get distracted no matter how hard I try to stay on task. But I did read the Psalms straight through one night. Every time I caught my mind wandering, I'd make myself start over."

"Hm. . ." Luke grew pensive. "What if you read, say, no more than ten verses every night, starting with the book of Matthew and afterwards wrote down on paper what they meant to you?"

Bethany shrugged. "I could do that, but suppose those verses don't mean anything to me? Suppose they're just describing something tiresome. . .like lineages and such?" The very thought caused her to stifle a yawn.

Luke grinned. "Write it down anyhow. Write, 'boring genealogy,' or whatever comes to mind after you read the passages. Then some time every day you can show me what you've got on paper. What you didn't understand, or what you found dull and uneventful, I'll try to explain and make interesting. Everything in the Bible is there for a reason."

"All right," Bethany agreed, partly out of a sense of obligation, but mostly because she struggled so in this area and secretly relished the thought of Luke helping her. "I only pray you won't discover what a hopeless case for a pastor's wife I truly am."

Luke chuckled. "I'll take my chances."

They exchanged a smile and an amicable silence lingered between them for a good stretch of road. Then Bethany spoke up.

"Luke, I'm sorry for my little temper fit earlier today. I didn't mean what I said about breaking our betrothal."

"I know you didn't," he replied easily. "Besides, I wouldn't allow you to break it—at least not like that, in the heat of anger. In order to get out of your promise to me, Bethany Stafford, either your father will have to pull rank or you're going to have to come up with a biblical reason for not wanting to marry me."

"That would make a fine case for me to study God's Word," she teased.

He tossed her a furtive glance. "Scamp."

Laughing, she turned toward him, admiring his rugged features against the backdrop of the setting sun across the desert plain. She realized Luke belonged here, in this wild territory.

"May I ask you something?" she ventured.

"You may," he said, grinning at her formal tone.

"Will you, um, tell me what you said to Catherine?"

"I reckon I can do that. Let's see. . .Catherine asked me if we were like-minded or some such thing."

"Actually," Bethany informed him in a matter-of-fact tone, "she said, 'Are you thinking what I'm thinking, Luke?' "

"You've got a good memory," he quipped. "And to Catherine's question, I replied that I thought it was late and time to turn in. I told her I had enjoyed catching up on family news, and I hoped she'd still be in the Territory when you and I got married so she could attend."

"You said that? What was Catherine's response?"

"She started to cry." Luke shook his head, wearing a sorrowful expression. "She told me she's lonely. She misses her dead husband. New Orleans, the city in which she was born and raised, has changed so much she scarcely recognizes anyone there. Her entire life has been completely altered because of the war." He paused momentarily, glancing at

Bethany. "Catherine said seeing me again was like a familiar link from her past."

"That's very touching, Luke," Bethany remarked dryly. "I can practically hear your heart breaking."

She couldn't help smiling at his sarcasm. "So did you succumb to her tears?"

"Me? No. A woman's tears don't impress me much. I've seen too many. I simply told Catherine I'd keep her in my prayers, but I wanted her to understand that I'm not a man easily swayed. Once I set my mind on something it takes divine dynamite to change it. I also let her know I made a commitment to you, Beth, and I intend to honor it no matter what."

"No matter what? I see."

Bethany nibbled her lower lip. She thought she should feel happy, but instead she felt remorseful. He was marrying her in order to spare her reputation in Silverstone and his sense of noble obligation had robbed him of his privilege of choice.

Commitment. The word thumped against her soul painfully. If she married for the same reasons as Luke, she'd have to marry Ralph Ames.

She recalled again spying him together with Catherine. She'd vividly seen the way Catherine had gazed up at him and she could just imagine Luke looking right back. Bethany sensed their attraction for each other. What else could it have been? And suddenly she could hear Richard's voice. . . .

"It may not be love yet," he'd said of the relationship between himself and Sarah. "But there is something between us. I'm sorry, Beth. I really am. But it's not meant to be for us. I'm sure about that much. And I love you, too—but as a sister in Christ."

"That could be enough—enough to start," Bethany had told him with tears rimming her eyes.

"That would never be enough," Richard replied emphatically. "And someday you'll thank me for my honesty. Someday when the right man comes along."

Shaking off the memory, Bethany focused her eyes on Luke. Was he the "right man," or was this another disastrous affair of the heart?

"You know," Luke said, "I need to do some apologizing myself."

"For what?"

"For kissing you this morning."

Bethany frowned. "What's there to be sorry about, Luke?"

"My impropriety, that's what. My father raised me a whole lot better than that. You don't belong to me yet, Beth, and I had no right taking such liberties with you. Why, if some cowboy-preacher did that to my daughter, I'd have him drawn and quartered!" Luke paused, gazing at her. "And I'd deserve it. Will you forgive me?"

"Of course," she said mechanically as her confusion grew. She hadn't ever kissed Richard, but after accepting Lionel's proposal, she'd allowed him an occasional show of affection—and he'd never apologized. Then, again, Lionel wasn't a gentleman like Luke. Moreover, he wasn't a man of God. Even so, Bethany couldn't help wondering if Luke had been politely telling her just now that he didn't enjoy kissing her, and therefore he was sorry about it. Maybe he was sorry about their engagement, too. Perhaps he was even sorry he'd ever brought her out west.

But in a way, she felt more remorseful than he could ever be.

twelve

Bethany scrutinized her reflection in the looking glass that stood in the corner of her bedroom. "It's so beautiful," she whispered, fingering the off-white dress Angie had given her. With its high ivory lace neckline, fitted bodice, and full skirt, Bethany decided the gown made her figure look quite womanly. Why, she might pass for twenty years old, instead of her real age of seventeen. But, of course, her appearance wasn't a concern to her. . .not anymore. She had no one to impress, certainly not Luke.

In the last day and a half, she'd come to a quiet acceptance about her betrothal to him. She expected the cannon ball to drop at any moment, but she had decided to do nothing about it. Instead, she was determined to concentrate on her upcoming teaching position. She would disciple Angie, help care for the Ames children, and wait. Luke would soon fall in love with Catherine and then he would attempt to gently tell her the news, just as Richard had, and Lionel, too. But this time, she'd be ready. She would trust the Lord for strength and protection; after all, He had bestowed His grace upon her many times during her journey west. And she wouldn't even cry when Luke severed their engagement. Then, after the shards of her broken heart were somehow restored by her Heavenly Father, and Catherine and Luke were married, Bethany would consider them good friends, seeing she loved Luke and felt a fondness for Catherine.

With a firm resolve, she studied herself in the mirror, thinking that in spite of it all, it would be fun to wear such a pretty dress to church. Besides, she'd promised Angie.

Bethany beamed, thinking about her brand-new sister in

Christ. Angie Brown was now a child of the King, a born-again believer.

Yesterday morning, Luke had walked Bethany out to the western ridge to visit with her friend. But Angie seemed so downtrodden, so sad. She talked about killing herself again, only this time, Bethany didn't think she could dissuade her from it and she called for Luke. He ended up speaking to Angie, encouraging her for half the morning, while Bethany sat beside him, praying silently. At last, with tears filling her blue eyes, Angie trusted the Lord Jesus Christ for her salvation, in this life and the next.

Then, later yesterday afternoon, Sheriff Montano entered the boardinghouse and secretly delivered this precious gift from Angie. A lovely new dress! But what made it special was the letter folded inside of it, stating that Angie had sewn the garment for herself before she'd given up on living a respectable life. *But because you befriended me,* she'd written, *and because of Christ, my hope has been renewed.*

It was certainly cause to rejoice!

Bethany began brushing out her hair, wondering what to do with it. She noticed the hot Arizona sun had branded golden highlights into several strands. Oh! if only she'd force herself to wear her bonnet, nuisance that it was!

She continued to toy with her hair, thinking the new dress demanded a different hairstyle, but what? She lifted the straight mane that fell to her waist just as a knock sounded on her door.

"Who is it?"

"Me, Catherine Harrison. May I come in?"

A knot gripped Bethany's stomach. "Yes," she replied haltingly.

Catherine entered wearing a pale peach gown. Her blond hair was expertly coiffured, giving Bethany a good moment of envy.

"Millie told me you've got a mirror. May I use it?"

"Of course." Bethany pointed to the object in the corner

and Catherine smiled politely. After several seconds of inspection, her gaze returned to Bethany. "I don't like to go out in public without making sure I look my best."

"You always look very lovely, Mrs. Harrison."

"Please, you must call me Catherine."

Bethany smiled and nodded, feeling more than a little intimidated by the woman. As pretty as she felt in her new pearly-white dress, her appearance could never compare with Catherine's exceptional beauty.

"What a lovely gown," she remarked.

"Thank you," Bethany replied demurely as she glanced self-consciously at her attire.

"You must share the pattern with me."

"The pattern?" She looked up, somewhat surprised, then shook her head. "A friend made this dress for me. I'm afraid I don't have a pattern."

"What a pity." Catherine circled her, her blue eyes narrowed in examination. "Your friend is a good seamstress."

"Yes, she is. It's my hope she'll return to that profession. . . soon."

"I see."

Bethany's discomfort grew under Catherine's fixed stare.

"You were about to style your hair," she observed. "Would you like me to help you?"

"Um, well. . ."

"I like to pin up hair and I'm quite good at it. Here, sit down. Let me try something."

Bethany lowered herself into the desk chair and Catherine stood directly behind her. Taking a handful of her long tresses, she wound it around one way, then another.

"You know, Bethany. . .may I call you by your given name?"

"Please do."

"Well, Mama always told me that a lady ought not grow her hair much past her shoulder blades. It's too hard to manage and it won't keep a curl. What would you say if I cut your hair for you?"

Bethany stifled a little gasp. "Cut my hair?"

"Just to there," she explained, poking Bethany gently between her shoulders. "We've got plenty of time before church begins. And afterwards, I'll pin it up for you."

"I don't know. . ."

"I'll get my scissors while you think about it."

Bethany rose and crossed the room, gazing into the mirror. Should she cut her hair? She'd never really thought about doing such a thing before. Sometimes her mother would trim the ends, but she never cut it. Wasn't her hair her glory?

Catherine returned in a flash. "What about it, Bethany?"

"Is it all right for a Christian woman to cut her hair?"

Catherine thought it over. "Well, to a degree, I suppose. We wouldn't ever want to wear it like a man. . .although I must confess, I've seen men with long hair. Why, there was a Yankee soldier in New Orleans who had shoulder-length golden curls that became the envy of every socialite in town!"

Bethany laughed nervously. "All right. Cut it."

"You're daring, aren't you?"

"I suppose I am."

"You would have to be, coming all the way out here to teach school. Well, all right, turn around."

Bethany complied, closing her eyes, praying Catherine could cut a straight line. Within minutes, it was done.

"There, see?"

"Oh, my! It feels so different." Turning, she inhaled sharply upon seeing all the hair on the bedroom floor. Then she looked in the mirror. Her hair looked the same, just shorter.

"Now I'll pin it up for you," Catherine said. "You'll find that your hair will be so much easier to work with since you've shed at least a foot of it."

To Bethany's surprise, the woman worked wonders, and as she pinned and looped, she explained how to make the French twist so Bethany could do it herself. When she finished, Bethany felt delighted with the outcome.

"You're a miracle worker!"

Catherine laughed. "Hardly, my dear." Taking the scissors in hand, she then snipped away at a few strands around Bethany's face. Wetting her fingers, she proceeded to create tiny ringlets. "There!"

Bethany stared at her reflection in awe.

"I think Luke will be very pleased with the results, don't you?"

At Catherine's statement, Bethany frowned.

"Oh, don't do that!"

"Do what?"

"Glower like that." Catherine put her hands on Bethany's cheeks and gave them both several gentle pinches. "When you frown, Bethany Stafford," she said, "it's as if a gloomy cloud settles over your face. But when you smile, you're quite pretty." Pushing her closer to the mirror, Catherine gave her cheeks another pinch.

"Ouch!"

"A bit of blush. . .now smile."

Bethany rubbed her sore face and felt like she couldn't produce a smile if her life depended on it.

"Come on now. Think of something humorous."

"I can't."

"Are you ticklish?"

"No. . .oooh! Stop that!"

"Yes, you are. Remind me to tell Luke about that little spot."

Wide eyed, Bethany spun around.

Catherine laughed gaily. "Smile, my dear, I'm teasing you."

Bethany conceded, but only to make Catherine stop her shenanigans.

"Ah-ha! I win. I made you smile."

"Yes, you did, Catherine." Bethany looked at her askance, her mind churning with plots and plans. Perhaps it wouldn't hurt to speed up the inevitable. "You and Luke would make a good couple," she announced carefully, "what with your teasing."

Catherine rolled her eyes. "I don't know about that. I think the two of you make a fine pair."

Bethany shrugged and moved from the looking glass. "I suppose. . ."

"You're not sure?"

She shrugged once more, then pivoted to face Catherine. "I just want Luke to be happy and sometimes I wonder if there's not somebody else who would make him a better wife."

Bethany purposely gazed into Catherine's eyes, wondering if she'd detect the subtle message beneath her words. But all Catherine did was smile and lay a sisterly hand on Bethany's shoulder.

"I believe it's normal to feel some insecurities before marriage. After all, it's a big step. Before our wedding, my husband Stephen would often say to me, 'Catherine, you could marry a far better man than I.'" A sad smile crossed her countenance. "Stephen wasn't wealthy and I came from money. But he was a godly man and a hard-working carpenter, so my father allowed the match." She sighed. "I loved him very much and we were so happy together."

For all her jealous feelings toward Catherine, Bethany's heart went out to her. "Luke told me he was killed in the war. . . I'm so sorry. But, perhaps, God has another husband waiting for you. Maybe someone just as godly. . .like a pastor."

Catherine's eyes narrowed suspiciously. "Now, Bethany, why do I get the impression you don't want to marry Luke?"

Turning away, Bethany paced a few steps. "It's not that I don't want to marry him," she began. Stopping and looking back at her, she added, "It's just that I'm not certain it's God's will."

"Hm. . .does Luke know this?"

Bethany felt her face growing warm with sudden discomfort. "Not really."

"You had better tell him, then. Oh, Bethany, don't hurt Luke. He's a good man, kind-hearted—"

"No, Catherine, I'd never want to hurt him. Not ever. I want him to be happy. . .with the right woman, and if it's not me, then I'm willing to step aside."

"How honorable," Catherine said sardonically.

Bethany shook her head. "No, not really. Perhaps it's quite selfish of me." She hadn't intended to share this much with Catherine; however, since she'd gotten this far, she decided to bare all—well, most of it anyway.

"You see, I've had my heart broken twice already and I don't intend to go for three times. Therefore, I want to be very sure it's God's will for me to marry Luke—because I simply cannot stand the thought of living the rest of my days with a man who doesn't love me."

Catherine produced a curt little laugh. "Luke wouldn't have proposed if he didn't love you, you goose."

"He would. . .and he did!" Bethany sighed. "Oh, it's a long story."

"I've heard his side, now I'd like to hear yours."

She sat down on the edge of the bed, and Bethany relayed the happenings of the past couple of weeks, including the reason behind their betrothal. However, she couldn't get herself to tell Catherine that she'd seen her and Luke together several nights ago. Despite her recent determination, it still hurt.

"Hm. . .I had a feeling Luke's strong-arm approach to proposing marriage could backfire on him," Catherine said, a little frown furrowing her delicate brows. "I told him as much."

"Yes, well, sparing a woman's reputation is a lousy reason to wed."

"Not really. In fact, something similar occurred to Luke's older brother, Benjamin. He rescued my dear friend Valerie from an awful mess in which she would have had to marry an unbeliever. Valerie's father made the match, and she would have rather died than marry James Ladden. Out of the two men, she chose Benjamin, and now he and Valerie are so much in love it's embarrassing." Catherine smiled reflectively. "It really was rather romantic."

Bethany lifted a derisive brow. "Are you telling me the McCabe men have a penchant for saving women and their reputations?"

Catherine laughed lightly. "Why, I'd never thought of it like that. Perhaps they do. Although, I cannot think of what Jacob would be saving Grace from. Spinsterhood if anything, for she vowed never to marry anyone but Jacob McCabe."

"But how did she know he was the one God chose for her?"

"She just knew and she waited on the Lord patiently until Jacob finally saw the light, so to speak."

"That's amazing. And here I've been deceived twice already." Expelling a discouraged little sigh, Bethany turned to the mirror and smoothed down her skirt. "I suppose it's probably high time we got to church."

"Yes, you're right." Then, as they both turned to go, Catherine caught Bethany by the elbow, adding, "I want you to know I won't repeat a word of this to Luke. It's your duty as his fiancée to tell him your concerns, although I believe they're unwarranted." The corners of her mouth lifted in a hint of a smile and her expression bordered on smug. "Luke isn't as noble as you may think."

Before Bethany could ask what she meant, Catherine propelled her out of the room.

≈

"Today I'll be preaching from the book of Matthew," Luke began from the pulpit, "verses one through seventeen."

Bethany sucked in her cheeks and bit down hard in an effort to forestall a laugh. *Boring genealogy.*

Luke had apologized twice yesterday for not beginning their Bible study as he'd promised; however, the funeral of the men killed in the ambush had produced various crises that needed tending. Bethany assured him she understood and, in truth, she'd felt relieved. She hadn't looked forward to sitting through a lecture on who begat whom. But it looked as though Luke meant to have his way regardless.

"Now before y'all go to sleep on me, I want to first explain the reason behind this book, and primarily these first seventeen verses. It was written by Levi, also known as Matthew, and it was a testimony to the Jewish nation, proving to them that Jesus Christ was and is the Messiah—the very One they'd been waiting for."

Luke began to read, pausing occasionally in brief explanation, and Bethany marveled at her ability to keep up with him. Her mind didn't wander. She understood. And by the end of the service, she felt almost excited about delving further into the Bible.

Luke made his way down the aisle while one of the elders closed in prayer. Then he dismissed the small congregation. As they left the church, they formed a line to shake hands with their pastor, ask questions, or exchange a few pleasantries. Since Bethany sat in the front pew beside Catherine, they were the last to leave.

"Will you look at that?" Catherine whispered over her shoulder. "That entire family is sound asleep. How rude!"

Bethany spied the object of Catherine's disdain: the Ames family. She inched forward, getting a closer look, and noticed that Ralph had shaved his beard. His shaggy light brown hair looked washed, his clothes clean, and his children looked bathed as well.

Then she saw little Michael, slipping ever so slowly out of Reggie's grasp. She apologetically pushed passed Catherine and gently lifted the baby from his sister's tentative hold. Reggie opened her eyes, smiled at Bethany, and closed them again.

"He kept us up all night," she murmured drowsily.

"Well, it's all right. I've got him now." Bethany gazed at the child, sleeping in her arms, and again that strange feeling came over her. Soon she found herself actually wishing Michael were her baby. In fact, she wished all these children were hers.

She peeked at Ralph from beneath lowered lashes. No, she couldn't do it. She couldn't marry him. True, he was a nice-looking man since he'd cleaned himself up, however, the thought of becoming Mrs. Ralph Ames left an unpleasant emptiness inside her.

"Sorry, baby," she whispered, kissing Michael's cheek, "I can't be your mama." She gazed at him, noting the soft lashes fluttering against pale cheeks, the perfect tiny nose, and wet rosebud lips. She decided Luke had been right. She was being overly emotional. But this boy had certainly captured her heart.

Bethany held him until the last of the church members had exited, Catherine included. Then Luke made his way back up the aisle to her.

He smiled.

She smiled back.

"Where'd you get that dress?"

"Angie gave it to me."

Luke's golden brows shot up. "That was nice of her."

Bethany nodded.

"You look right pretty in it."

"Thank you." Bethany fought against the oncoming blush. She didn't want Luke's niceties to affect her.

But they did.

"And you're especially lovely when you blush, too."

"Oh, Luke, you're incorrigible!" She rolled her eyes.

Chuckling softly, he turned his attention to the dozing Ames clan. He shook his head. "It's a sad thing to see what my preaching does to some folks."

Bethany laughed. "Yes, well, you'll be pleased to know your message didn't put me to sleep. I enjoyed it and everything made perfect sense. I now have an understanding of those verses thanks to you."

"Amen!"

His gaze met hers, and though he looked a bit chagrined by her compliment, she saw the tenderness in his eyes. Then, taking a deep breath, he glanced back at the Ameses.

"We've been invited to the Raddisons' for noon dinner. What do you suppose we ought to do with Ralph and his kids?"

Before Bethany could reply, little Jeb opened an eye. "Dinner? I'm sure hungry," he stated, stretching like a cat.

Jesse was the next to awaken. "Is service over? Oh. . . hello, Pastor Luke."

Luke nodded a greeting, and Bethany could tell he was trying to hide his amusement.

"Pa, wake up. Church is over."

At Jesse's prompting, Ralph roused and rushed into a series of apologies. Then he awakened the rest of his children.

"Sure am sorry 'bout that, Preacher. . .Miss Stafford."

He looked at Bethany, who averted her eyes, not wanting to meet his probing gaze. She lowered her chin and considered his infant son instead.

"All's forgiven, Ralph," Luke said. "Why don't you take your family to the Bakers' for dinner? Plenty of women there to help with the little ones and after a bit of a *siesta,* you're sure to be revived for the evening service."

"Reckon we already had our *siesta,* but I'll take the suggestion just the same. Oh, and Miss Stafford?"

Reluctantly, she glanced across the pew at him.

"Would you mind keepin' the baby for the afternoon? That'll give us something of a respite."

"Yes, I suppose I can do that."

"Much obliged." Ralph began making his way out of the church, his children following like ducklings. Then he stopped short and came back, standing in front of Luke.

"Preacher, I reckon I owe you an apology for my rude behavior a few days ago. . .well, truth is, I've been an ill-tempered man ever since you come back to town. It's on account of Elizabeth's death. I know that ain't much excuse for bad manners. You've been nothing but kind to me and my kids and I'm grateful to you in that regard."

"It's all right, Ralph. I know you're going through a trial."

The man took a deep breath. "But, well, I've got to add this, Preacher. I meant what I told you on my ranch a few days ago. It ain't no idle threat."

Luke pursed his lips but didn't reply, and Bethany watched with a mixture of curiosity and fear as the two men stared long and hard at each other. The air between them suddenly seemed to crackle dangerously.

Then Ralph turned his focus on Bethany and produced a quick smile. "Have a nice afternoon, Miss Stafford."

"Thank you," she answered warily.

Once he'd left, his children with him, all except Michael, Bethany turned to Luke. "What was that all about?"

"Aw, nothing."

"Luke?"

He tore his gaze away from Ralph's retreating form and smiled into her eyes. "Nothing you need to worry your pretty head over. Now let's get on over to the Raddisons' place. I'm starving!"

thirteen

"It's going to be a scorcher today, brother," Jacob said, entering the boardinghouse the following morning. Removing his hat, he mopped his forehead with a blue bandanna.

Luke grinned from where he lounged in the lobby after his morning stroll to the western ridge with Bethany. "Well, good morning to you, too."

Jacob cast him a doubtful glance. "And since when do you rise so early—or was this past week a fluke?"

"Bethany and I spend time together before breakfast."

"Ah. . .I knew there had to be a good reason."

Luke chuckled. "Come on and set a spell. Breakfast is going to be late this morning on account of some new arrivals last night. Apparently a river boat docked around midnight and soldiers from Fort Yuma, heading over to Prescott, disembarked and spent the night. So this morning Mrs. Baker is fussing up a storm for her new guests."

Looking warm and weary, Jacob accepted Luke's invitation and found a chair to occupy. "Where's Bethany now?

"Upstairs having some devotion time. She and I began our own Bible study."

"Studying as you stroll?" Jacob arched his brows.

"Naw, they're two separate occasions." Luke lowered his voice. "Main reason we take our early morning walks is so Beth can discreetly visit with one of the working girls by the name of Angie Brown. Beth made friends with her and a few days ago, Angie accepted the Lord as Savior."

"No fooling?" Jacob smiled, looking suddenly less tired. "Well, amen!"

"It's a blessing all right, but. . ." Luke sighed, shaking his head and feeling slightly hopeless. "Now we've got to figure

111

out how Angie can give up her, um, profession without getting herself killed in the process. She told Beth and me this morning that Chicago Joe has a mean hired gun named Jim. Ever heard of him?"

Jacob thought it over, then slowly shook his head. "Nope."

"Well, Angie said that if any of the girls get out of line or even hint at leaving, Jim beats them mercilessly. In fact, there have been several girls who've 'disappeared,' or so goes the explanation for their absence. But the rest of the girls know that Jim probably murdered them. Since they're right close to the river, Angie said it's likely he rendered those women unconscious and threw them in to drown."

"Lord, have mercy! Such wickedness going on right under our noses. As if the brothel itself isn't bad enough."

"And now we've got one of God's own in there," he stated bleakly.

"What do you aim to do?"

Luke shrugged. "Beth says I ought to convince Sheriff Montano to throw Angie in jail. She said I should tell the sheriff to dream up some charges that'll keep her in custody a while."

Jacob laughed. "That's a thought."

"Yes, but there's always a danger in involving another person. Besides, I've heard Montano makes personal visits to Chicago Joe's place. Could I really count on him to help us? Whose side is he really on?"

"I'll talk to him," Jacob promised. "Paden and I are on good terms. I'll be able to get a feel for the situation. And I'll do it without putting Angie in further danger."

"I appreciate that because, to tell you the truth, I've been at a loss for ideas since Beth and I returned from seeing Angie."

"Hm. . ." Jacob considered him. "And how are you and Bethany doing, anyway?"

Luke stood and stretched. "Fine, I reckon, but she can sure be a puzzle. This morning she seemed rather distant again— or maybe she just gets shy. I can't figure it out."

"She's young, Luke. Probably needs extra time. Think about it. Here's Bethany in this hot, Arizona Territory after living her whole life on a farm in Wisconsin. She's away from her kin for the first time. . .well, all that's overwhelming enough without adding the responsibility of a teaching position and an impending marriage."

"You're right. And I shouldn't even be pressing her about the marriage issue without hearing from her father."

"Well, from what you and Bethany have told me, I doubt he'll disapprove of the match. But I'd suggest you take your time with her, Luke. You're liable to scare the poor thing by coming on like a stampede as you're wont to do."

"Thanks, brother," Luke remarked dryly. He shook his head. "Stampede."

Jacob laughed. "I've got a feeling God's going to teach you patience yet!"

"Very funny."

At that moment, Luke saw Bethany making her way down the stairs in the company of Millie, Grace, and Catherine.

"And that's another thing troubling me, Jake," he whispered. "Since yesterday, Beth has been talking about Catherine as though she's some kind of goddess. Now, I'm right pleased they're getting along, but I've got this knot in my gut that says Beth is up to something." Seeing the ladies were promptly whisked off to assist the harried Mrs. Baker, Luke recounted Saturday's misunderstanding. "But I let Beth know I'm not interested in Catherine," he concluded. "Still, I sense the incident hurt our relationship."

"Well," Jacob drawled, "if we were back home in St. Louis, I'd suggest candy and flowers, but—"

"You're a big help. There's not a flower around for miles. Just parched sand."

"Oh, now, she'll come around. Be patient, Luke."

He sighed. "I'm trying. . ."

⋅≥⋅

Bethany thought breakfast was quite enjoyable, what with

the twelve Army officers in company. There was a lot of news out of Fort Yuma and Bethany watched as Paden Montano paid close attention.

"You heard about a particular outlaw gang, Sheriff?" one of the soldiers asked. "They've been robbing, looting, and murdering in towns and ranches up and down the river."

"Oh, my! I'm so frightened," Millie declared. Then she smiled at the officer sitting beside her. "But it is a great comfort to know such competent men are on duty."

Bethany cringed inwardly at the girl's flirtations.

"I think, perhaps, we should continue this conversation in my office later," Paden suggested. "I wouldn't want to upset the women who are present."

"Of course, and my apologies, ladies," the soldier replied. He looked to be in his mid-twenties. "I'm not accustomed to being in mixed company."

"There are no women at Fort Yuma?" Catherine asked.

"I meant civilians, ma'am. Mixed company as in civilians."

"Oh, I see."

The uniformed man smiled, and Bethany saw Catherine smile back.

"Are you residing here in Silverstone?"

Catherine shook her head. "I'm just visiting. I actually took up residence in Arizona City with my cousin Grace here."

"How nice. Do you like it. . .Arizona City, I mean?"

Catherine shrugged. "I'm not sure yet."

"She originates from New Orleans," Grace put in. She was as lovely as Catherine, although her hair wasn't as blond. Instead it resembled the color of honeycomb.

"I dare say life has changed for every one of us who live in the South," Catherine added.

"Sure has. I was born and raised in Atlanta, but moved to Pennsylvania when I was twelve," the soldier announced, as a rebellious lock of coppery brown hair fell down on his forehead. "I've still got family in Atlanta."

Catherine gasped with pleasure. "Really? You wouldn't happen to know the Sommervilles, would you? Harry Sommerville and his family? He practiced law."

"Of course, I remember them well!" The officer smiled. "Why, everyone in Atlanta knows the Sommervilles! My name's Wainwright. Lieutenant Wainwright."

"Pleased to meet your acquaintance, Lieutenant."

The conversation stayed light after that, until the captain in charge ordered his men to pack up.

"We best be heading out, too," Jacob said, looking at Grace, then Catherine.

"You're leaving?" Bethany asked incredulously. For some reason she'd been under the impression both ladies would stay in Silverstone until Grace and Jacob's wedding.

"You'll have to come and visit us in Arizona City," Grace told her. "But, of course, it won't be long and we'll be back for our special day." She looked over at Jacob adoringly.

Catherine expelled an exaggerated sigh and Bethany laughed. In a small way, she was sorry to see Catherine go.

❧

Later that morning, Bethany hugged the ladies good-bye.

"I'm glad to have met you," Catherine said with an earnest sparkle in her eyes. "I think you and Luke will be very happy together." Bethany gave her a skeptical little frown as Catherine added, "I'll be praying for you. . .for you both."

"Thank you."

"We'll keep you in our prayers, too." Luke said, stepping around Bethany. Then one by one he helped Grace and Catherine into the passenger wagon.

Minutes later, Jacob emerged from the sheriff's office and jogged across Main Street. "Sorry to keep y'all waiting," he said to the ladies. To Luke, he added softly, "Paden's willing to cooperate. Go talk to him."

Bethany understood his meaning, and Luke set a hand on her shoulder to still her mounting excitement.

"Thanks, Jake."

"Anytime, brother." He shifted his attention to Bethany. "Keep him in line while I'm gone, will you?"

"That's no small task, Jacob," Catherine retorted from the wagon. She glanced at Luke, her blue eyes twinkling mischievously.

He narrowed his gaze. "You know, Catherine, you Louisiana women sure have smart mouths."

Her jaw dropped indignantly. "Take that back this instant, Luke McCabe!"

"I will not. It's true!" He laughed at her outraged expression, adding, "And you've got no sense of humor, either!"

"Hmpf!" Feigning insult, Catherine whirled around on the bench, her white dress billowing like a cloud.

Jacob chuckled and climbed aboard the wagon, seating himself beside Grace. "See you in a few days," he called. "And maybe I'll even bring you back a telegram."

"You do that," Luke returned. "And, Catherine, I sincerely apologize if I offended you."

"You didn't. I know you better than that," she replied over her shoulder.

Smiling, he waved while the wagon pulled away from the boardinghouse and rolled out of town. His hand fell from Bethany's shoulder and she looked up at him.

"How 'bout we pay Sheriff Montano a visit?" He gazed into her eyes and a soft expression crossed his face.

Bethany looked away, wishing she hadn't seen it. Now that Catherine was gone, she'd have a hard time distancing herself from him. Yet she must if she meant to guard her heart.

"Beth? What do you say?"

She nodded. "Yes, let's go see the sheriff."

fourteen

Luke eased himself into a chair inside the adobe government building. "How much did my brother tell you?" he asked Paden.

"He told me nothing. I guessed. After all," he added, his thin, black mustache twitching, "I know our little school-teacher here has made friends with a certain young woman of questionable reputation."

Paden considered Bethany openly, wearing an expression of obvious fondness that set Luke's jaw on edge. But his jealousy dissipated somewhat when Bethany had the good grace to lower her gaze.

Paden turned and looked back at Luke. "I understand you two are betrothed. Millie Baker told me."

"That's right." Luke was more than happy to share the news with the sheriff.

"But it's not for sure," Bethany added, alarming Luke. "That's why we haven't made a public announcement. We're still waiting for my father to give us his blessing."

"Ah," Paden said with a slight grin.

Luke expelled a breath of air he didn't even know he'd been holding. He inwardly admitted Bethany was right, but at the same time it bothered him that she sounded almost relieved when she'd said, "It's not for sure." It was, after all, as sure as the dawn in his mind.

"Sheriff, we didn't come here today to discuss Beth and me," Luke finally stated. "We came here to discuss Angie."

Paden folded his tanned arms across his chest. As always, he wore a black cotton shirt, sleeves rolled to the elbows, and tucked into the waist of black pants. His long, dark hair was pulled into a ponytail that hung down to the middle of his back. "What about Angie?"

"Well, a few days ago, she accepted the Lord," Bethany informed him. "She's a believer now, and she wants to begin a new life—a decent Christian life. Consequently, she doesn't want to work for Chicago Joe anymore, but she's too afraid to leave because of someone named Jim who's liable to kill her if she tries."

"*Sí, chiquita,* he probably will," the sheriff agreed.

"But that's not fair!" She jumped up from her chair. "Angie has rights just like everyone else. She's entitled to quit a. . .a job if she chooses. And it's up to you, Sheriff Montano, to enforce her God-given liberties that our forefathers fought so desperately to obtain."

Paden smiled and sauntered over to Luke. "You know, my friend," he said, setting a hand on his shoulder, "I think you will have your hands full with this one."

"Yes, well, she'll keep life interesting." Luke sent an affectionate wink to Bethany.

"That she will." Paden chuckled and rubbed his neck in contemplation while he paced the floor. He stopped in front of Bethany. "So you think it's my responsibility to protect Angie?"

"Yes."

Again, Paden crossed his arms. "And what do you suggest I do in order to accomplish this obligation?"

"I think you ought to arrest Angie and put her in jail."

Throwing his head back, the sheriff hooted in a way Luke hadn't ever heard. "And what are the charges?"

"I don't know," she said defensively. "That's your department. You're the one who's supposed to know the law."

He chuckled again, but it ebbed like rumbling thunder fading in the distance. "I will think about it."

"Oh, but, Sheriff, there's no time. Angie's going to be forced to—"

"Enough!" Paden said firmly, holding up a hand to forestall further argument. Then he pointed to the door. "Out you go, Miz Stafford. I want to speak with the pastor privately."

She sighed in exasperation but left without another word.

Watching her flounce to the doorway, Luke felt a surge of pride mingled with admiration welling within his chest. The little sprite. But then she angrily slammed the door behind her, making him wince. That fiery temper again.

Paden let out a long, slow whistle while he stared at the closed door. "You know, pastor, there are times when I can not decide whether our little schoolteacher needs to be spanked or kissed."

Luke rose slowly, warily. "Neither, coming from you."

The sheriff seemed to consider the remark, before turning and facing him. "No need to be jealous, pastor, I won't pursue her, although I must admit I have thought about it. Until she came to town, I never pondered the idea of marriage. Now I think I would like to settle down someday with a woman who. . .how did you phrase it? She will keep life interesting? *Sí,* I want that kind of woman—one who is brave and undaunted, yet so innocent she blushes."

A sober expression spread across his shadowy features. "However, Miz Stafford's feelings for you are quite apparent and I'm convinced there would be no persuading her." He walked to a tall wooden cabinet which stood against the far wall and pulled out a long-necked bottle. "Can I interest you in some wine?"

"No, thanks." Luke inhaled impatiently. "Look, Sheriff, about this situation with Angie—"

"I have an idea." He stuck the wine bottle back into the cupboard, obviously unwilling to drink alone.

"An idea? Well, let's hear it."

He nodded. "But first, you must listen to a confession. I have, on occasion, patronized Chicago Joe's establishment, but I am not proud of that fact. Quite honestly, it causes me a good deal of shame."

"Sheriff, according to the Bible, you can confess your sin to the Lord Jesus Christ. You don't have to go through me."

"Yes, your brother has said as much; however, I am telling you this because I think we can use the sins of my past to good use." Paden sat on the edge of his desk, one leg dangling over the corner. "Here is what I propose. . . ."

ᶻᵃ

It seemed like forever before Luke emerged from Sheriff Montano's office. While waiting for him to cross Main Street, Bethany barely contained her curiosity at the outcome of their meeting. But he just sauntered on over to her as if he had all the time in the world.

"Luke, what happened?" she asked, meeting him at the edge of the sun-parched boardwalk.

"Everything's taken care of, darlin'." Taking her elbow, he steered her toward the boardinghouse.

"What do you mean? Is the sheriff going to arrest Angie?"

"Nope. He's got another plan."

"But—"

"But, nothing, Beth," Luke said firmly, yet quietly enough so they wouldn't be overheard by passers-by. "If you want Angie to get out of the brothel alive, you need to let Paden Montano take care of it. He knows what he's doing."

"He's going to rescue her, then?"

Luke gave her a subtle nod.

"When?"

"I can't tell you. . .now, honey, don't give me that disappointed look. It's for Angie's own good—and yours."

"Well, it's not like I'll blab it all over town, Luke," Bethany replied testily.

"I know. But the less you understand, the better."

"Can I at least say good-bye?"

"I figured you'd want to and the sheriff conceded to one letter. Write it this afternoon. I'll give it to him and he can pass it on to Angie. . .sometime."

They entered the lobby of the boardinghouse and Luke took off his hat, nodding politely to Mrs. Baker who waved a greeting from the midst of her company. Then he untied the red and white bandanna from around his neck and wiped away the perspiration.

"Will the sheriff get her out tonight?"

"I can't say. Furthermore, we are now changing the subject."

"Oh, Luke!"

Bethany felt like stamping her foot in frustration but stifled the desire since the army officers were about to take their leave. They stood around the Bakers, thanking them for their hospitality.

"What are your plans today?" Luke asked Bethany as the men left the building with Millie rambling incessantly in their wake.

Bethany shrugged. "I guess I'll finish unpacking books in the schoolhouse."

"Would you like to come out with me to the Bentleys' place? Ross Bentley's son was one of those men killed last week and I promised I'd help with some chores today around their ranch. But I'll bet Mrs. Bentley could use some female companionship about now."

"No, thank you," Bethany replied brusquely, still annoyed that Luke wouldn't confide in her. Besides, she didn't want to go anywhere with him. Why, he was likely to kiss her again and then apologize some more!

"Well, fine, you can stay here in town and be stubborn," Luke told her, wearing a bit of a grin. "And I reckon that's best anyhow. Since all the company is gone now, Millie is liable to need your undivided attention." Luke turned on his heal and walked out the door. "I'll see you this evening, Beth."

With arms akimbo, she watched him go. He drove a hard bargain. Either she spent this dreadfully hot afternoon with him, or she'd likely pass it listening to Millie chatter on about handsome soldiers and other mindless subjects.

"Luke!" she called, running after him.

He stopped in the middle of the boardwalk, looking back at her expectantly.

She caught up to him, panting slightly. "I changed my mind. I'll come with you."

He smirked good-naturedly. "I thought maybe you would."

fifteen

The afternoon dragged by as Bethany helped Mrs. Bentley with chores. A woman of fifty-some years old, Charlotte Bentley looked closer to ninety. Her sun-weathered face resembled a piece of jerked beef, and her wiry body hunched slightly forward. What's more, her leathery personality mirrored her physical appearance.

"Life's hard in the Territory," she told Bethany time and time again. "This part of the country takes life, doesn't give it. But we go on day in and day out just the same and all's it's gonna do is kill us in the end anyhow."

"Mrs. Bentley, you mustn't think that way," Bethany said in an attempt to console her. "God is as much in control out here as He is in Philadelphia. . .that's where you're from, isn't it?"

The other woman replied with an unladylike snort. "Yes, and I'd give anything to go back. I lost my five children out here. One to snake bite, two to cholera, my oldest worked for a freighting business in town and died trying to stop a saloon fight. He wasn't part of the brawl—just trying to do right!" Mrs. Bentley squared her drooping shoulders instead of shedding a tear. "And now Russell, killed in an Indian ambush. They're all gone and so will I be soon enough, I imagine."

Bethany sighed ruefully. How to encourage this woman? All it seemed she could do was go about her tasks as joyfully as possible, trying to think of something positive to say, even though Mrs. Bentley always shot it down with a pessimistic retort.

By the end of the evening meal, Bethany felt more than ready to climb into the wagon with Luke and head back to Silverstone.

"Well, thanks for all your help, Pastor," Adam Bentley said, reaching up to shake Luke's hand.

"You're more than welcome."

"And don't forget my offer. I hope you'll consider it."

"I'll do that. Thanks."

"And one more thing, Pastor. . . ." A remorseful expression crossed the aging man's face. "I sure appreciate your coming by today and I'm especially grateful for the talk we had out in the barn this afternoon. Reckon it helped put things in perspective for me, what with losing my youngest son and all."

Luke smiled graciously. "It was my pleasure, Adam." Reins in hands, he gave the mules' backsides a slap. "We'll be in touch."

As he drove off, Bethany grew curious. "What sort of offer did Mr. Bentley make you?" She paused, feeling suddenly chagrined. "Oh, forget I asked, Luke. It's none of my business."

He chuckled. "It's your business, all right. I don't mind telling you. Adam Bentley offered me a share of his homestead. He said there's an abandoned cabin on the north end of his property that his oldest son, Ronny, built, expecting to marry and raise a family in it. But he was killed during a mishap in Silverstone, and his fiancée up and married someone else and moved away. Cabin's been empty for nearly three years, but it's still standing as sturdy as ever. Adam wants me to share in the work and help drive the cattle to auction once a year and the place is mine. . .ours."

"What about your ministry?"

Luke shrugged. "What about it? I'll always be a pastor and there's no one stopping me from preaching on Sundays, whether I've got my own homestead or not. But I'll be honest, Beth, I'm right tired of working odd jobs. Even though I trust the Lord to provide for my needs—and for yours, once we're married—there's something inside me that longs to build a home of my own. One I can hand down to my son someday."

Bethany raised surprised brows and, though she didn't

reply, she wondered if Luke wasn't jumping ahead of things. A son? Why, they weren't even married yet!

"What do you think I should do?"

"I don't know."

"The Bentleys have some fine land, don't you think?"

She shrugged. "I'd prefer a farm with a cluster of lush green trees surrounding it, soft grass, and a garden full of colorful flowers instead of sand and more sand. . .and rocks."

Luke chuckled. "Getting homesick?"

"Maybe a little." Then she thought of returning to Wisconsin and the parents who'd rather see her on her own and caring for her own family. "On second thought, I'm not homesick at all."

"Good." He gave her hand a quick squeeze. "I don't guess I could let you go at this point. I love you, Beth."

Eyes wide, she fairly gaped at him. "You. . .you. . .do?"

" 'Course I do." He glanced at her, looking amused. "Why are you so thunderstruck?"

"B–because," she stammered. "I was under the impression you proposed simply to save my reputation." The harbored hurt and confusion suddenly came spilling out of her mouth. "Truth is, you seem to care about my reputation more than I do, and if getting married really provides the solution, I've been wondering if it wouldn't be a far better cause for me to become Ralph Ames' wife and for you to marry Catherine. She told me it would be easy for her to fall in love with you. She's so sweet—a perfect example of a godly woman."

"Hold on, Beth. I told you I don't love Catherine. Never will," Luke stated on a note of exasperation. "Now, get that notion out of your head once and for all."

Bethany sighed, wanting to rid her mind of the idea forever. "I can't help it, Luke. I didn't think you loved me and I've been worried that we're making a mistake."

"Mistake? You and me?" This time Luke looked stupefied. "Why, Bethany Leanne Stafford, I ought to take you over my knee. How could you think such a thing?"

"How couldn't I?" Folding her arms, she expelled an indignant puff of breath. "And for the record, if you ever take a hand to me, Luke McCabe, you'll be sorry."

His eyes widened at the threat before he turned his head and gazed out over the rutty road. Silence hung over them as somber as the encroaching dusk. Bethany felt like biting off her tongue. Here Luke said he loved her. . .why, this should have been a time of unforgettable romance, but she had to spoil it by throwing his words back in his face.

Then suddenly he began to laugh. The sound seemed to bubble up from deep within him until it erupted in a hearty chuckle that lasted for a good minute.

"I'm glad you think it's so funny."

"Aw, Beth," he said between chortles, "I'd never take a hand to you. That was a figure of speech. And you're one little spitfire." He sobered. "But I'm the biggest fool that ever walked God's green earth."

She gave him a curious glance. "What do you mean?"

"I mean. . .I've loved you since we left Missouri. Couldn't you tell?"

She shook her head, feeling foolish herself.

"I talked to my father about a possible match between us before we headed out for Independence, and the whole journey long, I prayed about it. I watched in a mixture of awe and delight as you shed your melancholy shyness for a quiet determination, then encouraged others along the way."

"That trip changed my life."

"I know," he said earnestly. "But you really couldn't guess at my feelings? I barely left your side for three months and only then when circumstances forced me."

"I noticed. . .but I thought you stayed close by only because you felt obligated to protect me."

He shrugged. "Reckon that was a good excuse, huh?"

Bethany smiled, shaking her head in wonder. "Maybe I had an inkling that you cared, but I never allowed myself to think about it much. Only after you proposed did I begin to consider how you might feel about me." She paused, examining her hands, folded in the lap of her colorfully printed skirt. "I've been hurt twice before, Luke," she confessed. "The first time, I mistook a young man's friendship for love, and the second, I rushed headlong into a relationship that resulted in a broken engagement."

He nodded pensively. "Before we left Wisconsin, Sarah mentioned you'd had a couple of heartbreaking ordeals, but she didn't tell me the details. I'd like to hear them if you're willing to share."

"All right." Bethany stopped momentarily to collect her thoughts. "Ever since I was about ten," she began, "my father talked about an arranged marriage between Richard Navis and me."

"Richard?" Luke's chin sprang back in surprise. "You and Richard? Sarah's husband? My brother-in-law?"

"The very same. You see, my father wanted to join the properties and build on them. But the war changed things. Marty Navis, Richard's father, came back from active duty maimed and there was talk of him selling their farm. My father convinced him otherwise, and we helped the Navises with chores. But Richard never wanted to get married. . .until Sarah came to town."

"And Richard fell in love with my baby sister," Luke surmised, "and threw a wrench into your father's plans—and yours, too, I expect."

"That's right."

"Were you in love with him?"

"I thought I was," Bethany admitted. "But as I watched Richard and Sarah's love blossom, I knew whatever I felt for him wasn't the same thing they felt for each other. Except I coveted what they had, so much so that I accepted the attentions of a young man named Lionel Barnes."

"Barnes?" Luke's brows furrowed slightly. "Why do I know that name?"

"Richard's cousin Lina married Lionel's older brother,"

Bethany explained. "You met them."

"Ah. . ."

She wrapped up the miserable tale by describing how Lionel had broken their engagement, claiming he didn't love her, and conceding to the fact he'd been merely using her as a convenient distraction.

"I'm sorry that happened," Luke said at last, "and I promise I'll never hurt you." He took her hand. "I really do love you, Beth, and not just as a friend or a sister in Christ, but as the young woman I hope to marry as soon her father gets around to giving me his blessing—which, I'm praying, comes soon."

She smiled, blushed, then gazed up into Luke's face in bold assessment. Could he really mean it? But one look at the sincerity pooled in his eyes and she knew it was true.

"Thank you for voicing your feelings, Luke," she said softly. "I don't feel half as insecure as I did an hour ago."

"And that's where I've been a blundering idiot. I should have told you right off. But, you see, I've been hurt, too. Reckon I allowed my own weaknesses to get the best of me, when I should have trusted the Lord. So when I saw the opportunity to propose marriage to you in a way you couldn't refuse, I seized it."

He relayed the story of how Miss Suzanna James, a St. Louis debutante, toyed with his affections, then rejected his offer of marriage.

"She turned you down?" Bethany asked incredulously, wondering over the woman's sanity. Couldn't she see Luke was a fine catch?

"Oh, she didn't just turn me down, darlin', she laughed in my face. Laughed hard, too. I was devastated and vowed never to try something as stupid as proposing marriage to a woman again!" He sighed. "Guess we've all got those areas of our flesh we need to give over to God."

Bethany agreed as Luke pulled the wagon to a halt in front of the boardinghouse.

"You up for some Bible study tonight?"

She nodded. "Looking forward to it."

"Good." Luke jumped down and then helped her to the ground. "I'll take the wagon to the stables and come back."

"All right." Bethany strolled to the boardwalk, then pivoted. The hot, arid breeze blew several strands of hair into her face and she brushed them back. In her typical fashion, her bonnet hung uselessly down her back. "Oh, and Luke. . .?"

"Hm?" He'd climbed back into the wagon and now peered down at her.

She crossed the distance to lean over the side. "I love you, too."

He grinned in a way she'd never seen before, sort of wistful and pleased combined. "See you soon," he promised.

Stepping back, she watched the wagon rattle by before making her way into boardinghouse. *Thank You, Lord,* she whispered in prayer, her heart filled with joy. Could this really be happening? She and Luke. . .in love. . .planning to marry? The world seemed suddenly wonderful, and for once even the Arizona heat didn't bother her.

Now, if she could just be sure of Angie's safe escape from Chicago Joe's wicked establishment, everything would be perfect!

sixteen

At first, Bethany felt disappointed when Millie imposed on the Bible study later that evening. She had wanted Luke all to herself. But, it soon became apparent the girl struggled with reading and comprehending God's Word, too, and Bethany felt guilty for her selfishness.

Luke read Matthew chapter one, verses eighteen through twenty-five.

"I've got a question," Millie piped up once he'd finished. "Why did Joseph have to 'put away' Mary if they were engaged? Doesn't that mean he wanted to divorce her? But they weren't married."

"I'm glad you asked that," Luke said with an encouraging grin. "Keep in mind what I told you yesterday during the church service. The Book of Matthew was written primarily to the Jewish folks and, according to Jewish custom, an engagement was as binding as marriage. To get out of it, a divorce—a putting away—had to take place, and that's what the Bible is referring to here. Mary told Joseph she was expecting a child, and he knew it wasn't his, so he considered breaking their engagement, or putting her away."

"You are ever so smart, Pastor Luke," Millie gushed.

And you are ever so flirtatious, Bethany wanted to say, although she bit back the remark. She supposed that as a pastor's wife, she'd have to learn how to minister to other Silly Millies in the world. *Lord, help me love her.*

"Bethany," Luke asked, pulling her out of her thoughts, "what did you write down after reading these verses today?"

She opened her leather-bound journal. "I penned a paragraph about Mary's trust in God. It struck me as quite profound. I guess I hadn't ever thought of her as a real person in the midst of a potentially scandalous situation. Yet, there she was. . .unmarried, expecting a child, and her betrothed wanted to break their engagement." Bethany glanced at Luke. "In other words, Mary had good cause to fret, but the Bible doesn't indicate she did."

"That's right," Luke said. "Mary was submissive to God's will. In the Gospel of Saint Luke, she states. . ." He flipped through the pages of his Bible until he found the verse. " 'Behold the hand maid of the Lord; be it unto me according to thy word.' "

Bethany marveled at the woman's faith and wished hers could be just as undaunted. How freeing it would be to simply let God handle every crisis, comfort every troubled thought. And why couldn't He? God is the same now as He was in Mary's time. It occurred to Bethany that the hindrance lay within herself and her fear of trusting Him with every aspect of her life here on earth.

The Bible study ended and Millie looked appropriately thoughtful. After asking a few more questions, she excused herself and went upstairs for the night.

"You know, Luke," Bethany remarked as they walked toward the doorway of the boardinghouse, "I think studying God's Word has been good for Millie tonight." She flushed slightly. "For me as well."

"I'm glad to hear that, although I must admit God convicted my heart about few things."

"Oh?" Bethany gave him a curious look. "How so?"

"Trust, for one thing—or my lack thereof." Luke shook his blond head, looking disappointed in himself. "Beth, I sure wasn't trusting the Lord when I coerced you into marrying me. Catherine even warned me that I had. . .how'd she put it? 'Strong armed' you into accepting my proposal. But my intentions were good. I was just plumb scared you'd turn me down."

"Like that woman did years ago?"

Luke nodded. "Like Suzanna."

A somber moment passed between them and then Luke's gaze brightened.

"Beth," he said, placing both hands on her shoulders and leaning toward her, "wait right here, all right? Don't move. Promise? I've got to fetch something, but I'll be back."

"All right," she replied hesitantly, wondering what in the world Luke was up to now.

She waited fifteen minutes before he returned, wearing a look of apology.

"I'm sure sorry about the delay. My mother gave me something before we left St. Louis and I forgot about it till now. But then I had to remember where I packed it away."

Bethany smiled weakly, still confused.

"Anyway, I found it."

"Good."

Luke grinned. "And now I aim to do this right." He straightened his black leather vest that covered a white cotton shirt, and then, much to Bethany's amazement, he got down on one knee.

He took her hand. "Beth," he began, "I love you. Will you marry me?"

She wanted to laugh and cry at the same time. "Oh, Luke. . ."

"Well?"

A little giggle escaped her. He certainly was the ever-impatient man. "Yes, I'll marry you."

Luke stood to his feet. "You just made me the happiest man in the Territory."

A full laugh erupted. "Oh, Luke, I already told you I'd marry you."

"Yes, but now I actually gave you a chance to get out of it."

Bethany shook her head at him.

Then Luke pulled out a round golden brooch with a large pearl in its center. "Will you accept this as an engagement gift? It was my grandmother's."

Bethany accepted the proffered heirloom and examined it thoughtfully. "It's lovely," she breathed. She looked up at Luke and smiled into his blue eyes. "I shall treasure it forever."

He returned her smile before expelling a reluctant-sounding

sigh. "I reckon we'd best call it a night. Morning comes awfully fast."

Bethany agreed. Then, impulsively, she raised herself on tiptoes and planted a kiss on Luke's mouth. He responded, his arms encircling her waist, but in the next heartbeat, he gently pushed her away.

"Beth, we ought not be doing that," he explained, looking disappointed. "It's not right. You don't belong to me yet."

"You don't like kissing me?" She felt wounded.

"I love kissing you." He chuckled, adding softly, "In fact, I enjoy it more than I have a right to. But there'll be plenty of time for kissing after we're married. I promise."

Reluctantly, she nodded. "I'm going to hold you to that, Luke McCabe."

He laughed. "You won't have to, darlin'. But it's high time for me to be leaving." He crossed the room and grabbed his wide-brimmed hat. "Good night," he told her, his gaze holding hers for a long instant.

" 'Night, Luke."

Bethany watched him go, feeling as though her heart went with him. And suddenly, she couldn't wait to become his wife.

❧

The cool morning breeze blew against the skirt of Bethany's light blue dress as she waited for Luke. She simply had to see Angie one last time. With one hand, she fingered the brooch at her throat, while glancing down at the folded parchment in her other. Bethany hoped it wasn't too late to give her newest sister in Christ the words of encouragement she'd penned very late last night. But if Luke didn't hurry, they'd run out of time. He should have been here by now.

Growing anxious, Bethany strolled to the end of the street where the little clapboard church stood proudly facing into town. Behind it was Luke and Jacob's quarters. Walking up to the door, she knocked.

"Luke?"

No answer.

She turned the knob and stuck her head into the tiny place. It appeared neatly kept, although it was hardly homey. A dirt floor. No glass panes in the windows, just crudely carved wooden louvers devoid of curtains. Dark blankets were thrown across the straw mattresses on the two beds. But Luke was nowhere in sight, and of course Jacob hadn't yet returned from Arizona City.

"He forgot," she muttered irritably. Spinning on her heel, she marched back to the boardinghouse, silently complaining to her Heavenly Father. *Lord, how could Luke forget? He knew I wanted to say good-bye to Angie and it's all his fault I didn't get a letter over to the sheriff yesterday afternoon, since he took me to the Bentleys'!*

Reaching the Bakers' establishment, Bethany waited a bit longer, hoping she'd see Luke emerging from one of four directions. However, Main Street was quiet this time of morning. Businesses were still locked up tight. Even the sheriff's office had a large "Closed" sign posted on the outside of the door.

Jail must be empty, Bethany mused absently. Then she remembered the sheriff was going to rescue Angie. Perhaps he was doing that right now! She bit her lower lip. Maybe Luke and Sheriff Montano were at the western ridge at a planned rendezvous and they'd soon be assisting Angie in her escape from Silverstone!

Excitement made her pulse quicken as she clutched the letter against her breast. Oh, if only she could help and say good-bye to Angie in the process!

In the next moment, her mind was made up. She would walk out to the ridge and meet them all. No doubt there would be something she could do to aid Luke and the sheriff in securing Angie's departure.

With purpose in each stride, Bethany headed toward the other end of town and made her way along the familiar rocky pathway. Arriving at the ridge, she found it deserted with no signs of anyone having been there this morning.

Suddenly she heard a decisive click coming from somewhere

behind her. Slowly, she turned and peered in horror at the gun leveled at her, and then at the scruffy man holding it.

She gasped.

He sneered. "Well, well, lookie here what I found." His light brown shaggy hair matched the color of his matted beard. He turned his head and called to a friend, "Come see what I got, Digger!"

While the man holding the gun watched his comrade approach, Bethany surreptitiously removed her brooch and slipped it into the sleeve of her dress. She felt certain she had run into two-bit outlaws and once they discovered she had nothing of value, they'd set her free.

The man called Digger came into view. He was fair-headed and appeared much less unkempt than his companion.

"Whadda ya think?"

"Boss won't like it, Mal." Digger said.

"Boss don't gotta know. I aim to have my way with this little thing and then I'll kill her."

Digger shrugged. "Well, just be quick about it. I don't want Montano on our heels."

Bethany inhaled sharply. This couldn't be happening! Only too late, she remembered Luke's warning her not to come to the ridge alone. She groaned inwardly. Any tragedy that befell her now was because of her own blunder.

The man leered and came toward her.

Think quick, Bethany, she told herself. *Oh, Father God, help me please!*

He inched closer, a diabolical gleam in his eye.

"Montano?" she murmured. "Do you mean the Sheriff Montano?"

He paused.

Digger, too. "What about him, missy?"

"Well, he's on his way here." Bethany hoped it was the truth. "I was going to meet him."

Both men gaped at her, then Digger's face reddened in anger. "You got Paden Montano's woman, you fool! He'll kill us fer sure!"

"She ain't his woman. Look at her. Why, she looks like a. . . a schoolteacher!"

"I am a schoolteacher!"

"Well, what do you know?"

"Turn her lose, Mal. We got enough demons riding our backs. And if she's some kind of acquaintance of Montano, she's not worth the trouble."

The man named Mal considered Bethany through narrowed eyes. "Maybe we can strike a deal. A pardon in exchange for the sheriff's sweet schoolteacher here. He'll want his woman back."

"But I'm not his woman," she quickly fired off. However, she immediately realized that her life meant nothing to these men unless she meant something to Paden Montano. "I'm. . . I'm his sister," she lied desperately.

"Right." Digger hooted. "And I'm Robert E. Lee." He rapped his partner on the shoulder. "I reckon she's his woman, after all. We'll take her with us and then send a right fine message to the good sheriff. I 'spect the boss won't mind us coming up with a plan of our own fer once."

Mal's jaw dropped slightly as an indignant expression crossed his mangy face. "I found her and I mean to have her."

Bethany shuddered in disgust. Glancing around, she wondered how she'd ever manage to escape. There seemed no way out. Behind her a steep cliff descended sharply. Jumping meant certain death, but perhaps she'd prefer it to enduring the profound depravity lurking in the minds of these two obvious outlaws.

"Take her. I don't care," Digger said. "But wait till we strike a bargain with Montano. Then you can deliver up his woman. . .only she'll be dead."

They laughed wickedly and Bethany stepped backward until she leaned up against three large boulders standing to the side of the embankment. The middle one stood at least five feet high. Mal, with his gun still drawn, strode toward her and grabbed her arm.

"Get your filthy hands off me!" Bethany cried, pushing

him away with all her might. She no longer cared if he shot her. If he planned to kill her anyway, she'd fight him to the death.

Mal sneered and she slapped his face with her one free hand.

In retribution, he used his gun to strike a blow to her head, and she fell to the ground. Her vision blurred and then she was jerked roughly to her feet. She swaggered slightly.

"Do that again and I'll put a bullet right through you."

"Go ahead," she replied, tasting blood, "because I'd rather die than let you touch me!"

Wearing a furious expression, Mal pressed the cold metal gun barrel hard against her cheek and Bethany braced herself for the inevitable. It was comforting to know she'd soon be in the arms of her Savior, although her heart ached for Luke. He said he loved her and to lose her on account of her own stupidity was more than tragic. It was downright senseless! *Lord, forgive me!*

Suddenly, Mal's gaze moved up over Bethany's head, and the look on his face turned to surprised terror. He raised his gun, aimed, fired, but not before an arrow caught him square in the chest. Bethany was thrown to the ground as gunshots exploded around her. She lay there, tense and unmoving, until all was deathly quiet.

Ever so slowly, gingerly, she lifted her pounding head. Her jaw ached terribly where she'd been hit. She scanned the scene before her. Mal was obviously dead—Digger, too, an arrow protruding from his neck.

Standing to her feet, she turned cautiously and found a coppery brave watching her.

"Warring Spirit."

"Preacherlukemccabe's Woman," he replied without any expression.

Was she safe now? Bethany didn't know. Could she trust this Indian man? But in that moment, it didn't seem to matter. Her knees gave way as the world spun crazily around her until it disappeared within a blanket of murky blackness.

seventeen

A sense of foreboding came over Luke when Bethany didn't show up for breakfast that morning. Millie announced she wasn't in her room, and Rosalinda hadn't seen or heard her leave. After he finished his meal, his apprehension increased when he looked for her in the schoolhouse but didn't find her there. She wasn't in the church either. Next, he walked through town and checked with folks. No one had seen her.

Finally he headed for the sheriff's office.

Paden looked up from his work. "What can I do for you, *amigo*?"

Luke sat down in one of the chairs, scraping it up to Paden's desk. "I don't know how to say this, Sheriff. I don't want to say what I'm thinking."

Curious, Paden gave Luke his full attention. "Say what?"

"Bethany's missing—and I have a sick feeling she went out to the western ridge alone, hoping to find Angie there."

"You didn't tell her our plans to put Angie on the steamer this morning?"

Luke shook his head. "I didn't want her to fret, and I especially didn't want her trying to. . .help."

Paden grimaced. "Ah, I see what you mean. Well. . ." He rubbed the back of his neck. "Did you ride out to the ridge?"

"No. If she hasn't returned by now, something's happened."

The sheriff waved off his concern. "Knowing our little schoolteacher, she's found another woman like Angie to take under her wing. Check the brothel." He laughed.

"This isn't funny." Luke tamped down his frustration and got to his feet. "I'm worried."

"I understand, Pastor." The sheriff nodded and rose from his chair as well. "How about if she does not show up by noon, I will ride out with you and investigate."

Luke reluctantly agreed, although he decided to saddle up and do his own searching. . .now!

"Sheriff! Sheriff!" A man burst through the door. "Sheriff," he panted, "two of our ranch hands were found dead this morning at the western ridge. Indians got 'em."

"How do you know it was Indians?" Paden asked.

"They had arrows sticking in 'em, and if that ain't an obvious sign of Indian attack, I don't know what is!" He shook his head. Then, noticing Luke, he peeled off his hat, revealing sweat-matted auburn hair. "Oh, g'mornin', Pastor."

Luke nodded. "Seth. Good to see you again."

"Likewise." The man turned back to Paden, his light brown eyes filled with concern. "Mr. Buchanan is awful mad. He says you'd better do something, Sheriff."

"Where are the bodies now?"

"I buried 'em just outside of the Buchanan property line. In this heat and all. . .well, it seemed like the best thing to do."

"And the names of the deceased?"

"Jack Smith and Joseph Johnson."

"Never heard of them."

"They rode onto Buchanans' property 'long about a month ago. Drifters, I 'spect. Said they'd done gold digging in California, served in the Confederate Army, and didn't have families to speak of. We were short-handed and, as the foreman, I hired 'em on."

"And the arrows? Where are they?"

The man frowned. "Huh?"

"I might be able to tell the band of Indians who killed your men if I inspected the arrow shafts."

"Oh, well. . ." The foreman shifted uncomfortably. "I done buried them, too."

Paden sighed and folded his arms, looking weary. "Tell Clayt I'll ride out this afternoon."

"Right, Sheriff."

Seth left and Paden shook his head. "How are you at

exhuming graves in one-hundred-and-twenty-degree heat, Pastor?"

Luke grimaced. "Never did it before, but I reckon I can dig as well as any man."

"Good. Let's take a ride to the western ridge and look for our little schoolteacher. Then we'll head for the Buchanans' place. I will help you, if, *por favor,* you will help me. Deal?"

"Deal," Luke agreed, albeit reluctantly. The job sounded grim at best. However, he owed the man a favor for getting Angie safely out of Chicago Joe's den of iniquity.

During the wee hours of the morning, Luke had waited with a wagon hitched to a team of mules in the shadows of the alley behind the brothel. He had prayed the entire time that he would remain unseen, and God answered his request. Meanwhile, the sheriff paid his money to "spend time" with Angie and once in her room, they'd tossed down her belongings, then climbed out the window to the awaiting buckboard. Next, they drove to a secluded dock Luke never knew existed. It had been used by the Confederates years ago. There, a captain-friend of Paden's waited for Angie to board his river steamer. Paden had previously explained that Angie was a "good friend" who had gotten herself entangled in a "most unfortunate situation," so the captain kindly agreed to waive the ninety-dollar passenger fee and promised to see her safely onto an ocean vessel at the mouth of the Colorado River.

"Anything for you, Paden," he'd said. "You saved my life once, and I'm forever indebted to you."

A short while later, the steamer set off down the river with Angie waving good-bye from the upper deck.

"Thank you," she called. "I'll never forget you—either of you! And tell Bethany I'll miss her!"

Now, shaking himself from his reverie, Luke threw a glance at the sheriff. "Didn't think you'd call me for a favor so soon."

Paden lifted his shoulders. "If you must know, I cannot

stand the sight of dead men. I detest the smell of death."

"What?" Luke felt like laughing. "You're one of the best guns in the Territory."

"*Sí.* I have no trouble killing a man if duty warrants it," Paden admitted. "I just do not enjoy the scene afterwards. It is a peculiarity with me."

"I reckon so. A squeamish lawman. . .imagine that." Half amused, Luke turned and headed for the door.

"Oh, and one more thing. . ."

"Yes?"

Paden's face was a mask of sobriety. "If your beloved truly ventured to the ridge this morning as you suspect, we may not find her alive. Drifters? Indians? It does not look promising." He expelled a long breath. "Perhaps I should ride out alone after all."

Luke shook his head. "No. I want to come."

With that he left the government building, his heart heavy within his chest.

⅜

Bethany moaned and opened her eyes. She focused her gaze. "What are you doing here, Reggie?"

"I live here."

"Then what am I doing here?"

"Warring Spirit brought you. Don't you remember?"

"Vaguely."

Bethany recalled awakening on the horse and feeling a pair of strong arms around her waist, but her head had hurt so badly she must have lost consciousness once more.

"You've got a nasty gash on the side of your head," Reggie informed her. "Your pretty blue dress is bloodstained. But I've got it soaking."

"Thank you," Bethany said weakly, closing her eyes.

Then she remembered.

"My brooch!" She bolted upright and her head throbbed. She groaned.

"Lie back down, Miss Stafford. You need to rest."

"But my brooch. Luke gave it to me. I put it in the sleeve."

"I didn't see it, Miss Stafford. Honest. Now lie down before Pa comes and sees you in your chemise."

Bethany gasped and settled back against the pillows under the light-weight quilt.

Reggie grinned impishly. "I knew that'd make you rest."

"You sassy thing."

The girl giggled and set a cool compress across Bethany's forehead. The hammering behind Bethany's eyes ebbed slightly, but the thought of having lost the brooch made her feel worse somehow. She wondered if Warring Spirit had found it.

"Why wasn't I taken back into town?" she demanded irritably.

"Oh, Warring Spirit would never set foot in Silverstone. Why, he'd likely cause a riot. Most folks hate Indians—and vice versa, I reckon."

"Then I imagine it's a special blessing that your father has managed to befriend him."

"I don't know if they're friends. They trade things. Like today. Pa traded his best horse for you."

"What?" Bethany ripped the cloth off her forehead and gaped at Reggie. "He shouldn't have done that!"

"He had to," she explained, "otherwise Warring Spirit said he'd sell you to some other Indians."

"And here I was beginning to think he was a decent sort."

Reggie shrugged and forced Bethany to reapply the cool, wet rag to her head. "Warring Spirit doesn't like whites, but he's not a bad Indian, either. And he doesn't understand our ways. For instance, he calls you Preacher Luke McCabe's Woman, but he sold you, figuring Pa would make you his woman now."

"I guess I owe your father a horse."

"Maybe you could marry him instead," Reggie suggested hopefully. "All of us kids love you, Miss Stafford, and Pa's tryin' real hard to be nice lately."

"Oh, dearheart, it just can't be. I love Pastor Luke." She peeked at Reggie and saw her crestfallen expression. "I'm sorry."

"Well, just rest now, Miss Stafford." Reggie sounded forlorn. "There'll be plenty of time for talking later."

ᕫ

"What did you find, Pastor?"

Luke glanced at the sheriff, then back at the brooch. "I gave this to Bethany last night," he fairly choked in reply. "Her betrothal gift."

Paden groaned. "Did you look over the cliff?"

Dread filled Luke at the suggestion, but he managed to shake his head in answer. "Reckon I need to do that."

Sí, amigo.

Luke walked to the edge of the ridge, squeezed his eyes closed and prayed, *Please, Lord, don't let me find Bethany lying dead in the ravine.* Opening them, he scanned the side of the bluff, the rocky arroyo below. . .nothing.

He returned to where Paden stood. "Praise God, she's not there."

"That may be unfortunate."

Luke frowned. "How so?"

"If Indians have her, depending on which tribe—"

"Stop, Sheriff. I've heard all the horror stories."

"Very well. Shall we continue our search?"

Luke nodded, pocketing the brooch, and mounted his horse.

ᕫ

"Mr. Ames, I really do feel much better," Bethany fibbed. "Could you please take me into town? The children are asleep and Reggie can listen for them."

"Ain't safe to leave her alone out here at night—and riding through the desert after dark is just askin' for trouble." Ralph folded his arms looking stubborn.

"But I don't want Luke to worry about me. When he finds me gone, he'll worry."

"I don't care much about that preacher's state of mind.

Now pipe down before you wake the baby," Ralph muttered. "Last thing I need is him cryin' all night long."

Bethany clamped her mouth shut.

"Git along to bed now. I'll sleep in the barn."

She hesitated.

"Go on!"

At last she acquiesced. Wouldn't do any good to stand and argue with the man. Furthermore, he was right. Leaving Reggie and traveling at night would be dangerous.

Ralph left and she shed her blue dress, which had dried nicely in the arid afternoon wind. Her head throbbed mercilessly and she climbed back into bed, wondering about Angie. Was she safe? Her thoughts moved to Luke. Was he fretting over her whereabouts?

"Dearest Lord Jesus," she whispered into the darkened cabin, "I cannot help Angie, but You can. I hold her up to You in prayer. And, Father, You know Luke's mind much better than I could ever hope to. Please give him peace concerning my absence. Keep him safe."

The pain in her head ebbed as she continued praying silently. *And, Lord, I do ask for these precious Ames children. Please find them a mother and. . .well, perhaps it's not nice of me to ask, but I pray You will do something about their father's dour temperament!*

Bethany finished her petition and closed her eyes. She suddenly recalled something Luke had said during a Sunday morning service while they were on the trail. He'd said, "After we pray about our worries and fears, we've got to give them to God and trust He'll take care of them. He said He would, and the God of the Bible never breaks His promises."

Searching the corners of her mind, Bethany tried to remember the passage of Scripture Luke had recited to back up his statement. Had it been from Philippians? Ephesians? She sighed. She'd have to ask him. In the meantime, she would hang on tightly to her faith. After all, if God could save her soul, He could do anything!

eighteen

The Buchanans' ranch was the finest in all the Arizona Territory. The house was a two-story wooden structure furnished with luxuries from back East that most people in this part of the country had long forgotten. Thick velvet draperies shaded glass windows, carpets matted the hardwood floors, and Mrs. Buchanan served her guests tea from delicate china cups and saucers. Of course, such niceties wouldn't last long if the Buchanans hadn't employed armed guards who roamed the far corners of the estate, protecting the family from renegade Indians and bandidos. However, Clayton Buchanan could afford it, and Luke listened intently while the man relayed his gold mining tales of how he'd struck it rich back in '62.

"That story is right impressive, sir," Luke replied at last. They had just finished supper, and now he glanced around the dining room where they sat at the large, polished table. "This whole house is mighty fine. . .and, Mrs. Buchanan, you served up a tasty meal tonight."

"Well, thank you, Pastor," she replied demurely.

Luke thought of thanking her for donating books to the school, but he felt sick with grief over Bethany's disappearance, and he couldn't bring himself to utter the words.

"Men," Clayt said, looking first at Luke and then at Sheriff Montano, "shall we retire to my study where we can discuss business?"

Luke shuddered inwardly. The business that needed attending was grisly, at best, and hardly a subject matter he looked forward to deliberating on a full stomach.

Paden, however, acquired a sudden burst of gumption. He rose. "The sooner we get this over with, the better. The preacher and I have a long ride back into town and it's already dark."

"You're welcome to stay the night," Clayt offered as they ambled into his study.

"I think not."

"Suit yourself."

Clayt called for his foreman, Seth Patterson, then closed the door. "Brandy, gentlemen? Cigars?"

Luke declined, but Paden joined their host and accepted a small snifter and lit a fat cigar.

"I reckon this is sin, eh, Preacher?" Clayt inhaled deeply of the rolled tobacco.

Luke merely shrugged. "It's sin if your heart convicts you."

The older man lifted his dark brows curiously, and Luke thought he resembled Ulysses S. Grant, with his walnut-brown hair and full, well-groomed beard. "You mean to say I ain't gonna hear a sermon about my diabolical ways?" He chuckled cynically and swallowed his brandy.

Sitting in a high-back leather chair, Luke crossed a booted foot to his opposite knee. "I 'spect you're old enough and smart enough to know right from wrong. Don't need me to spell it out for you. Although," he added with a wry grin, "if you'd like to hear me preach, you're welcome to come to church on Sunday."

From the chair beside him, Paden chuckled, his dark mustache twitching, and Clayt smiled.

"You know, Pastor, I think I like you," Clayt said at last. "You sure ain't one of 'em holier-than-thou ministers whose collars are as stiff as their very souls." The man snorted. "Why, I might even think about coming to your church—it'd sure please my wife."

"You do that, Mr. Buchanan."

A knock sounded on the door and Clayt boomed a "Come on in!" It opened, revealing the red-headed foreman.

"You wished to see me, sir?" Seth quickly eyed Paden and Luke, giving them a perfunctory nod.

"Set yerself down, there, son. Brandy? Cigar?"

Seth waved off the offer.

"Well, then, let's get down to business." He turned to his foreman. "Seems our hired hands weren't who we thought."

"Oh?" Seth frowned and turned suddenly wary. "How's that?"

"The sheriff and pastor, here, dug 'em up this afternoon, and—"

"Dug 'em up?"

"Nasty business, I know," Clayt continued with a grimace. "But Sheriff Montano had to do his investigatin' and he discovered those men were actually two outlaws he'd run out of town a number of times."

"Imagine that," Seth replied evenly.

"Their names," Paden added in his slight Mexican drawl, "were Horatio or 'Digger' Tabers and Malcolm DeWitt, also known as Mean Mal. They are part of a gang of cattle rustlers who have been thieving and murdering up and down the river. I suspect they are responsible for the Buchanans' loss."

"Impossible. I say Indians done it. Besides, I'd know if my own men were stealing from our stock."

Paden shrugged.

"And how do you account for the arrows that killed our guards?" Seth continued.

"White men can learn to shoot a bow and arrow."

Seth stood and angrily squared his shoulders. "You always defend them Redskins, Sheriff." He looked at his employer. "You ain't gonna get no help from the likes of him." He turned back to Paden. "And how do you explain the arrows that killed them two? More white men?"

"I inspected the arrows. From their markings, I believe they come from a clan of Yuma Indians. They are disgruntled with white men and have been known to do battle, but they fear extinction of their people more than they care about stealing cattle and murdering for no reason. I am willing to bet your men were killed in self-defense."

Looking at Clayt, Seth replied, "You see? He takes the Injuns' side."

"Did it ever occur to you that he knows what he's talkin' about?" Clayt asked in a sarcastic tone. "And them two dead outlaws may have had partners who did the actual cattle rustling on my ranch a couple weeks ago."

"That is correct," Paden said. "Tabers and DeWitt did not work alone. I'm sure of it. But there is another concern: a young woman—Silverstone's new schoolteacher. She has disappeared and may have been abducted by the gang—or the Indians who killed the two men you buried today, Patterson."

"Merciful heavens!" Clayt looked aghast.

Luke sighed and sent up a prayer for Bethany's safety. Had the two outlaws found her? Had they harmed her? Did their gang members really capture her—or did the Indians save her life before riding off with her? And, if the latter was true, had she been hurt. . .or worse? Luke's mind whirled with possible scenarios, each one more painful than its predecessor.

❧

Bethany awoke to find little Jeb had made his way into her bed and curled up next to her. His younger sister Lorena had done the same and lay nestled against her on the other side. Sandwiched between the youngsters, Bethany was reminded of how she'd slept with her siblings and how they'd kept each other warm during the frosty Wisconsin winter nights. But today in the Territory, cuddling proved much too warm. Even now, in the early morning hours, Bethany could feel her still-aching head soaked with perspiration.

Carefully rising from the bed, so as not to disturb the children, she gasped when she saw her blood-soaked pillow. She gingerly touched the wound behind her ear and discovered it had reopened. Her fingers moved to her hair, which was stiff and matted.

"I must look a sight," she muttered.

She dressed quickly and quietly. Then, pail in hand, Bethany made her way to the riverbank and fetched some cool water in which to wash. Coming back up the hill, her heart pounded and her vision blurred so much she had to sit down in the stony path and collect herself. She realized the blow to her head yesterday had done more damage than she'd first thought.

Her lightheadedness abated and she rose, climbing the hill to the cabin once more. She made it, feeling weak and nauseated.

"What's the matter with you?" Ralph grumbled as he entered the cabin. He looked crabby and Bethany wondered if he hadn't slept well out in the barn.

"I think I need a doctor, Mr. Ames," she said. "My wound opened up and I don't feel good. My head hurts and I nearly swooned while bringing in water just now."

"Nonsense. You'll be fine. Can't rightly baby yerself because of a little scratch on yer head and bruise on yer cheek. Besides, Doc Ramsey is miles away."

Bethany shut her eyes against the onslaught of frustration. "I am not in the habit of babying myself, Mr. Ames, but I know when I'm ill." She sighed, deciding it was pointless to argue with the man when he'd denied his own wife medical attention.

"Mr. Ames, if you won't get a doctor, would you at least hitch up your team and take me back to Silverstone?"

"Mrs. Canton comes out today to help with the children and chores around the house," he replied irritably. "You can ride back with her later on." He shook his head. "Why is it you women are always so sickly?"

Tears filled Bethany's eyes, but she turned away so Ralph wouldn't see. She wasn't "sickly." She'd simply got the sense knocked out of her yesterday. Why couldn't he be kind and understanding?

She thought of Luke and decided he'd be sympathetic. . .if he were here. She wondered if he was worried. "I really need to get back to town soon," she stated in the strongest voice she could find. "By now I must be missed. I don't want to alarm anyone."

"I ain't makin' a special trip into town, so git that outa yer head! I've got work to do!" He paused before adding, "And you owe me for the loss of one of my best horses."

Bethany swallowed hard. "My father gave Luke some money for my needs. Perhaps there's enough left to buy you a new horse."

"I don't want a new horse. I said I wanted the loss repaid. What I need is a wife."

"Do you really think the two are in the same category, Mr. Ames?"

"Aw, now, I didn't mean that. Haven't I tried to be nice and gentlemanly around you?"

She shrugged. "I guess you have seemed more. . .polite, yes."

"Well, that's because I want you to reconsider marrying the preacher and marry me instead. I even told him as much. What's more, God spoke to my heart and said you were the one to become the mother of my children."

Thinking of baby Michael, Bethany fairly gulped. "B–but I love Luke. I can't marry you."

Ralph glowered at her remark. "Then make me some breakfast. You can surely do that much."

"Mr. Ames, my head hurts so badly I can hardly think. And, while I appreciate your hospitality, I am not your maid. You'll have to make your own breakfast today. . .either that, or wait for Mrs. Canton to arrive."

Bethany instantly regretted her strong words. When she saw the fire in his eyes, she feared she'd gone too far.

But Ralph didn't so much as raise a hand to her, even in warning. He just stood there, looking petrified and infuriated all at once.

"You've got one unbridled tongue, missy," he said at last, "and a rebellious spirit to match. But I confess, there's something about you that makes me want to take you to wife all the same. Maybe it's me who needs his head examined by Doc Ramsey."

Bethany didn't know what to say, so she said nothing. After several tense moments, Ralph stomped out of the cabin. Tearfully, she began washing the blood out of her hair.

❧

The Cantons showed up by mid-morning with their brood in tow, and Margaret looked horrified when she discovered Bethany in such sickly condition. Bethany explained how she'd done the most foolish thing by walking off by herself yesterday and how she ended up here.

"He exchanged a horse for you? Hmpf! I'm surprised Ralph did that much. But you do need a doctor," Mrs. Canton agreed. "I'm going to have Joseph drive you to Doc Ramsey's place. Take my daughter Amanda with you. She's quite a little helper."

"Thanks, but I don't want to inconvenience your husband."

"Oh, hush. It's no inconvenience at all. And Ralph should have done this yesterday, that ignorant excuse for a man." She sniffed. "Pardon me, dear. That wasn't very. . .Christian of me, was it?"

Bethany just smiled a reply while Margaret went to the opened cabin door and hailed her husband from the barn.

After hearing the situation, Mr. Canton willingly agreed to get Bethany the needed doctoring. He assisted her into his wagon and Amanda climbed into the back. Reggie protested, saying she should go and help tend Miss Stafford, but her father hushed her, saying she had chores around the ranch.

Disappointed, Reggie stepped onto the wagon to give Bethany a good-bye hug. "I don't know why Pa is so ornery today," she whispered apologetically. "He's been trying to be such a good pa lately, too."

"It's all right," Bethany assured her. "I'm going to be fine. And after a good night's sleep, your father will feel better."

But as Mr. Canton drove off the Ames' property, Bethany couldn't help wondering if she'd just told another lie.

nineteen

The day passed agonizingly slowly for Luke. Before noon, the sheriff rode out to a Yuma village he knew, insisting the Indians would be more cooperative if he went alone. The waiting nearly killed Luke. But by late afternoon Paden returned with disappointing news: He hadn't found any sign of Bethany and none of the Indians claimed to have seen her. Luke wondered if they lied, but Paden said he got the feeling they were being honest and nothing had seemed amiss in their camp.

Alone in the cabin he shared with his older brother, Luke broke down. With tears flooding his eyes, he poured his heart out to the Lord.

"Why, God?" he cried. "How could You allow this happen?" He knew Bethany's disappearance wasn't the Lord's fault, yet his flesh longed to blame the One who controlled heaven and earth.

Jacob came home then, and with one glance at Luke, he paled. "What's wrong, brother?" He looked as though he were almost afraid to know.

Luke forced himself to communicate the grim events of the past twenty-four hours, but he didn't feel much like having company at the moment. He wanted to be alone with his grief and suffering, only Jacob wouldn't allow it.

"Self-pity set in already, eh?"

"Back off!"

"Not a chance. God brought me home at this moment, and you're going to talk to me even if we've got to slug it out first."

"Don't tempt me."

"Throw your best punch." A lock of Jacob's blond hair fell over his forehead and his brown eyes glinted with challenge.

"Come on. . .if it'll make you feel better."

Luke grunted out a weak laugh. "I'm not fighting you, Jake."

"Well, good, 'cause I'd win anyway." He relaxed visibly. "Now start talking!"

"All right." The dam of anguish suddenly burst. "I'm angry with Beth for wandering off when I told her not to, and I'm angry with myself for not stopping her. I could have informed her of the plan to get Angie out of Chicago Joe's place, but I didn't want her to worry. And I'm powerful angry with God."

"Easy, Luke."

"Easy?" He frowned at his brother. "How could God let this happen?"

"You know as well as I do that God allows bad things to happen but they're mostly human nature's doing. Except we know all things work together for good to them that love God, to them who—"

"Shut up! I cannot abide Romans 8:28 right now."

Jacob shook his head ruefully. "Where's your trust, Luke?" he asked gently. "Where's your faith?" Stepping forward, he placed a hand on his brother's shoulder. "You trusted God to bring you safely across the desert, over the mountains, protect you from snake bite and Indian attack, but you can't trust Him with the woman you love? What's that, huh?"

A lump of emotion filled Luke's throat and tears brimmed his eyes. "You're right," he choked. "I know God is good always, whether in trials or times of rejoicing. I preach on that subject frequently. He's my God! My Savior! He saved me from the pit of hell when I was six years old, yet here I am, behaving like one of the devil's own." He fell to his knees. "Forgive me, Heavenly Father. . . ."

Jacob's hand remained firmly on his shoulder, and when at last Luke stopped sobbing, he glanced up and apologized to his brother, too.

"I got no right to be a pastor."

"You're a fine pastor." Jacob's own eyes were moist, although he smiled warmly. "You're just flesh and blood like everyone else."

Emotionally spent, Luke could only nod.

"Listen, why don't you and I take a ride and scout around the ridge?"

"Did that already."

"Well, let's do it again. But this time, we'll prayerfully ask God to show us where Bethany is."

"I asked Him to show the sheriff and me yesterday," Luke replied.

"Ask again, brother," Jacob said. "Only this time ask believing the Lord will answer you."

Finally Luke agreed to saddle up and search for Bethany. His faith continued to wane, but he confessed his unbelief to the Lord as soon as it surfaced. "Lord, I believe; help thou my unbelief," he mentally recited from Mark 9:24.

Mounting his horse, he followed Jacob to the edge of town where they met up with Joseph Canton and his family.

"Say, Pastor Luke, I got a message for you!"

Reluctantly Luke reined in his horse, but only because Jacob stopped. He'd been tempted to throw the folks a neighborly wave and continue riding. He was too worried about Bethany to make small talk.

He forced a polite smile. "What's the message, Joseph?"

"Came from Bethany. She said to tell you all that's happened and not to worry. She's at Doc Ramsey's now."

Luke was too thunderstruck to speak. Jacob laughed heartily.

"God sure is good, eh, Luke?" his brother asked between chortles. "We didn't have to search too far before He led us to Bethany's whereabouts."

Luke gave Joseph Canton his undivided attention now. "What happened?"

The tale unfolded, leaving Luke weak with gratitude.

"The doc said she likely got her skull cracked, so he and

his missus are keeping her at their place to rest a while. But she's young and strong and gonna be just fine real soon."

"Much obliged, Joseph. . .and, Mrs. Canton, I'm sure glad you showed up at Ralph's when you did."

"You're welcome, Pastor."

The Cantons pulled away, their children waving from the wagon, and Luke turned to Jacob.

"I reckon you can guess where I'm headed."

"Yep." He scrutinized the horizon. "You have a couple hours of daylight left. If you ride hard and fast, you might just make it before sundown."

Luke nodded. "See you tomorrow."

Steering his horse around, he took off in a gallop, only to hear his brother calling him back. He halted once more. "Now what?"

"I almost forgot to give you this." Jacob pulled a folded note from his inside vest pocket. He grinned broadly. "It's a telegram."

&

"I know you don't feel hungry, dear, but you need to eat to regain your health. This venison stew is sure to perk you up."

Hesitantly, Bethany opened her mouth, took the proffered spoonful of food, chewed, and swallowed. "Mm, that's good, Mrs. Ramsey."

The woman smiled, looking pleased, and Bethany accepted another mouthful. It occurred to her then that she hadn't eaten all day.

"You've been so kind to me. . .your husband, too. Thank you."

"Oh, you're welcome, dear."

While Bethany ate, she studied the woman who insisted upon feeding her as though she were an infant. Snowy-white hair, pulled back into a graceful chignon, framed pink cheeks that were lined with age. Her eyes were a snapping bluish-green color and from their depths shone a gleam of spunk, perhaps even mischief.

"There, now, you're all finished and ready for a good night's sleep."

"I'm not sleepy."

"You will be. I've been instructed to give you a spoonful of this medicine. Open up. That's a girl. You're sure to rest easy with that in your system." Mrs. Ramsey set the dark brown bottle next to the empty dishes and lifted the tray. "Good night, dear."

"Good night," Bethany replied with a slight smile as she watched the kindly woman march out of the room. Then, closing her eyes, she slept.

❧

"Now, Pastor, I'll not have you waking up my patient!"

"I won't, Doc. I promise." Luke stood on the front porch of the elderly man's home where he and his wife sat enjoying the cool night air. Luke respectfully held his hat in his hands. "I won't disturb her. I just want to see with my own eyes that she's all right."

Dr. Ramsey rose slowly. "Very well," he muttered, sounding somewhat irritated. "Come along."

Luke followed him into the cabin's main room that served as a parlor, dining area, and kitchen. To the left, the Ramseys had built on a private bedroom that also incorporated the doctor's make-shift office. Toward the back, they had added a lean-to for his patients, and that's where Luke found Bethany sleeping peacefully.

"Satisfied?" Dr. Ramsey asked curtly, holding up the lantern.

Luke nodded. "I never doubted your doctoring ability, just my own faith."

The older man seemed to soften and put a hand on Luke's shoulder. "Now, son, she's going to make a complete recovery." He grinned. "You got special feelings for the new schoolteacher?"

"I sure do. Fact is, we're betrothed. We just haven't made it public knowledge yet because we've been waiting on her father's blessing. It came today."

"I see. Well, I reckon that explains your persistence."

Luke stepped into the room and knelt by Bethany's bedside.

"But I mean it, son," Dr. Ramsey whispered in warning, "don't you wake her up and especially don't rile her. She needs to rest that wound."

Luke inclined his head in silent acquiescence. Then, taking Bethany's hand, he lowered his chin reverently and whispered a prayer of thankfulness. Opening his eyes, he saw her drowsy gaze upon him.

"Luke. . ."

From behind, he heard the doctor expel an exasperated breath. "Shh, Beth, it's all right. Go back to sleep."

She gave Luke's hand a gentle squeeze. "Please forgive me for going out to the ridge after you said not to. I was looking for Angie. I didn't think about what you said. . .until it was too late."

"Shh, darlin', all's forgiven and Angie's well on her way to San Francisco by now. There's nothing to worry about. You just rest, else Dr. Ramsey's going to tan my hide."

"Might do that anyway," the elderly man mumbled.

Bethany's lashes fluttered, as though she fought to stay awake. Raising her hand, Luke pressed a kiss to her fingers.

"Go to sleep. I'll see you again in the morning."

"Wait," she insisted, tightening her hold on his hand. "I've got to tell you something. I did an awful thing."

"What's that?"

"I. . .I lost your grandmother's brooch." Fat tears pooled in her sleepy gray eyes. "I took it off and tried to hide it so—"

"I've got the brooch," Luke quickly assured her. "I found it at the ridge when the sheriff and I went looking for you. It's safe. . .and so are you. Just rest now and heal up."

She nodded.

Luke stayed with her a few more minutes until her breathing deepened. Finally, he stood and faced Dr. Ramsey.

"She's asleep."

The doctor nodded and led Luke out of the room. Back out on the porch, Luke sighed deeply and slumped against the doorjamb.

"That young woman took fifteen years off my life!"

Dr. Ramsey chuckled. "Yep, women'll do that."

His wife inhaled sharply. "Why, William Ramsey!"

"Aw, now, I'm just funnin' with the good pastor here."

Mrs. Ramsey replied with an indignant "Hmpf!"

Luke grinned. "Would it be much trouble to put me up for the night? I can sleep just about anywhere."

"I think that can be arranged. What do you say, sweet pea?"

Mrs. Ramsey rose from her chair. "Of course there's room for the pastor. It'll take me but a moment to throw a bed together. Excuse me."

Stepping aside, Luke allowed the woman to pass. "Thanks, Doc, for everything."

"Oh, you're welcome, son. Why don't you set a spell and we'll talk some."

"I'd enjoy that."

Taking Mrs. Ramsey's vacated seat, Luke leaned back. For the first time in two days, he allowed himself to relax.

twenty

True to his word, Luke planted himself beside Bethany's bedside first thing the next morning.

"I hate that ugly bruise on your cheek," he said ruefully. "I think I hate it more than the bandage around your head."

"I suppose it's the least of my consequences for disobeying you. My injuries could have been much worse. God protected me—and taught me quite a lesson in the meantime."

"I reckon so. Finish up your breakfast, now," he told her.

"Oh, please don't mother me, Luke. It's bad enough that Mrs. Ramsey treats me like a child."

"All right, all right." He smiled, although it didn't quite reach his blue eyes.

"What's wrong?"

"Oh, I've been thinking. Stayed awake half the night dwelling on a particular matter." He sat in a wooden chair, his hands folded and dangling between his knees. Lowering his gaze, he considered them thoughtfully. "I don't guess I'm called to be a pastor after all."

"What?" Bethany frowned in confusion. "You're a wonderful pastor. Since I met you in Milwaukee last October, I've learned more about my Heavenly Father and it's all because of your teaching."

"Well, that's nice of you to say, but—"

"And what about all those people who traveled with us as far as Santa Fe? You cared for their souls, Luke. Remember? After little Justin died from that rattlesnake bite, you led his parents to a saving knowledge of Christ. And what about the kids who fancied my rubber ball biscuits? They're on their way to Heaven because you cared enough to share the gospel with them. Then there's Mr. Bentley. . .remember how you encouraged him just the other day?"

"God can use anyone, Beth. I'm nothing special."

She gave him a curious look, feeling oddly alarmed. "Why are you questioning your calling?"

"Beth, I don't have an undaunted faith like my father or brothers, Benjamin and Jacob. I was right panicked when I discovered you missing yesterday."

"I thought you might be. Oh, Luke, I'm sorry."

He waved away her apology. "God was testing my faith and I failed."

Nibbling her lower lip, she wished she could think of a biblical illustration involving some other godly man who failed God. She had only been a Christian for a few years, yet she'd been raised in the church. She recalled hearing the Bible preached from the pulpit, but it used to bore her. She had viewed the Word of God as a tiresome Book that only a scholar could discern, and she hadn't seen salvation as a necessity for her own soul until Richard confronted her about it. She then accepted Christ as her personal Savior shortly before her fourteenth birthday. *Oh, Father-God,* she prayed *wistfully, why didn't I pay more attention to Your Word? I could use the knowledge of it right now.*

She remained pensive for a long moment. Finally, she looked at Luke, noting his expression of misery, and asked, "Who said, 'O wretched man that I am'?"

"That'd be Paul in his letter to the Romans—chapter seven, I believe."

"Yes, of course. Paul. He's considered one of the greatest apostles, isn't he? Why did he call himself a wretched man?"

"Because he knew his flesh was as wicked as any unregenerate man's." Luke smiled kindly. "I know what you're getting at, darlin', but it ain't the same."

"Why not? We all make mistakes. Every one of us has the flesh to contend with and we fail God from time to time. But if we confess our sins, He readily forgives us, correct?"

"That's right."

"And then we're all the wiser for it afterwards."

Luke's smile broadened. "You know, Beth, you'd make a good preacher."

"No," she replied emphatically, "I think I'll just marry one instead."

Luke snapped his fingers. "That reminds me. The telegram. . ." He pulled it from his shirt pocket. "Jacob gave this to me yesterday. It's from your father. He's given us his blessing."

"I knew he would." Bethany happily took the slip of paper and read it over. "Shall we set a wedding date?"

He nodded, his features brightening. "How's this afternoon sound?"

ða

Much to his dismay, Luke was forced to wait for over a week. It took Bethany half that long to recover from her injuries and another few days to make wedding plans. Hasty invitations were delivered to townsfolk and ranchers alike, including Sheriff Montano, Harlan Whitaker and his wife, the Bentleys, Ramseys, and Buchanans, as well as Luke's entire congregation. Jacob, who planned to perform the ceremony, rode into Arizona City and fetched Grace and Catherine so they could partake in the festivities also.

At last, the day arrived.

"It seems you and Luke have settled your differences," Catherine remarked, helping Bethany dress for her wedding. Bethany had decided to wear the dress Angie had given her, since she hadn't had time to sew a new gown.

"Yes, we did. . .oh, Catherine! I love him so much!"

"He loves you, too. It's quite obvious." A bittersweet smile lifted the corners of Catherine's pink lips. "I prayed for God's will. . .for both of you."

Bethany pulled her into a hug filled with both gratitude and consolation. *Someday, Catherine,* she thought, *that lonely void in your heart will be filled.*

When Bethany finished with her attire, Catherine lovingly pinned Grandmother McCabe's brooch to her gown, and they set off for the church. They'd barely arrived when Mrs. Raddison began plunking out the wedding march on the piano. Bethany walked down the aisle behind Millie, her one and only bridesmaid, and fixed her gaze on Luke. He stood tall and handsome near the altar, with Adam Bentley, his misty-eyed best man, beside him. As she came nearer to him, Bethany saw that Luke looked hot and nervous. Observing his discomfort somehow calmed her jangled nerves.

They spoke their vows, and then, fearing Ralph Ames would jump out of his pew, Bethany held her breath when Jacob said, "If anyone knows why this couple should not be joined in marriage, let him speak now or forever hold his peace." To her relief, not a word was uttered.

Finally, Jacob announced, "Luke, you can go ahead and kiss your bride."

"Hallelujah!" Luke declared. Gathering Bethany in his arms, he kissed her thoroughly while the onlookers applauded.

Afterward, a small reception line formed at the door to accommodate the well-wishers. Millie giggled incessantly, especially as the sheriff sauntered through the queue, but Bethany felt too happy to mind.

Paden shook Luke's hand, then moved to Bethany. "I hope you are very happy, *chiquita*." He lifted her hand and placed a kiss on her fingers.

His mustache tickled and, embarrassed by his boldness, she pulled away. Glancing at Luke, Bethany caught the subtle warning in his eyes as he watched the sheriff walk away.

"What a rascal," Luke muttered. Then he smiled and accepted congratulations from the next guest.

The Ames family brought up the end. The girls hugged and kissed Bethany, and the boys shook Luke's hand like little men, all except baby Michael, of course, who slept soundly in Reggie's arms.

Finally it was Ralph's turn. He nodded curtly to Luke, then pointed a callused finger at Bethany. "You still owe me the loss of a horse and I aim to call you for a favor. A big favor."

With that, he stomped out of the church.

"What was that all about, son?" Adam Bentley asked, standing next to Luke.

"I'll explain later."

"Right-o."

The older man gave him a fatherly rap on the shoulder. Ever since Luke accepted the Bentleys' offer to share their homestead, Adam had all but adopted Luke as his own. And Charlotte Bentley had been clucking over Bethany like a mother hen for the past three days. With their own parents so far away, Luke and Bethany were grateful for the older couple's affection—and God seemed to be using the younger couple to heal the Bentleys' wounded hearts.

The wedding party ambled out of the church and headed for the boardinghouse, where Mrs. Baker was serving cake and punch.

"Hold on, Beth." Luke slowed his pace and allowed the others to pass them. When Millie and the Bentleys got a fair distance away, he backtracked and steered her around the cabin he had shared with Jacob up until today.

"Where are we going?"

"Home."

"What? But I thought we were joining everyone else."

"Trust me, sweetheart."

Within moments the wagon came into view. It was hitched to a team of mules, and Bethany saw Jacob loading up the last of their belongings.

"You owe me one, brother."

Luke chuckled. "I know, but your turn is coming soon enough."

Jacob grinned and placed a kiss on Bethany's cheek. "Welcome to the family, sister."

"Thank you," she said demurely just before Luke hoisted her into the buckboard.

"By now you may have noticed that Luke's mighty impatient. At his insistence, Grace and Catherine packed your things right after the ceremony," Jacob explained. "And I threw all of his possessions together. Reckon you two are all set to commence the homemaking."

Bethany felt herself blush as Luke climbed up beside her. After a wave to his brother, he slapped the reins and the wagon lurched forward, heading toward their new life together on their recently acquired ranch.

epilogue

Journal Entry: July 30, 1867

Luke and I have been married for a whole month now and I have never been happier. If there were any lingering doubts in my mind regarding my husband's love for me, they vanished after our wedding night. Luke was—and is—tender and passionate with me, and I have discovered I can be quite ardent in return. At first I feared I was wanton and sinful, but Luke assured me that God ordained love between a married couple at the beginning of time. God said it was good.

My Bible reading is advancing nicely. Presently, I am studying Matthew 28, the Great Commission. I have begun to realize one of the processes our Lord used to teach His disciples so they could go out, preach the gospel, and make disciples of all nations. That process involved tests of faith— and God uses it to this day. When I mentioned my theory to Luke, he agreed and added that true faith is like true love, it grows stronger with time and experience. My husband is such a romantic!

Our cabin is comfortable. It has four large rooms, wooden floors, and glass windows—a far sight better than many cabins in the area. I have been working diligently to make it homey. I purchased material and sewed pretty curtains and a matching table cloth. Last evening we invited the Bentleys over for supper, even though we see them almost every day. I am pleased to report that Mrs. Bentley's spirits have improved greatly. Luke said the reason is because I have shown her the love of Christ, but I think she is just glad to have some neighbors and another female with whom to talk and sew.

Journal Entry: August 12, 1867

Jacob McCabe and Grace Elliot are finally married, and it's quite a feat, since I never saw a more nervous groom in all my life. Hours beforehand, he paced our cabin floor, saying, "Forever is a long time, brother. Maybe this isn't such a good idea." Luke told him that poor Grace had waited patiently for him for years and now he had better do right by her or else. "Besides," he added, "married life is a wondrous thing. You'll enjoy it, Jake. I promise." It greatly pleased me to hear Luke felt that way.

After Luke performed the ceremony, Jacob relaxed considerably, although he still wore a doomed expression, and I cannot fathom what came over me, but I could not stop giggling all afternoon.

Journal Entry: September 12, 1867

I have suspected it for some time, but now I am certain: I am expecting a baby! Luke is overjoyed and dotes on me constantly. He says he is sure the baby will be a boy and wants to name him Joshua Luke. I told him I would like to overcome my sickness in the morning before I think about names.

School should have begun by now, but due to my poor health in the morning, I have been forced to postpone teaching. Many of the people in Silverstone are unhappy with me and said they figured this would happen if they hired a woman to teach school. Their irritation distresses me as I never intended to renege on my responsibility.

Journal Entry: September 14, 1867

I have been crying all evening. Luke came home from a meeting in town and said I will no longer be Silverstone's schoolteacher. Catherine Harrison is going to replace me. She will be moving into the cabin Jacob and Luke once occupied. It seems the town's residents do not mind that Catherine is a woman, which seems quite unfair as they held my gender against me—and more so now, since I am in the family way.

I feel heartbroken. I came to the Arizona Territory for the sole intent of teaching school, but Luke said I came out here to marry him and raise his babies. I grit my teeth as I pen that last sentence. Sometimes my husband can be such a. . .man!

Journal Entry: September 29, 1867

I helped Catherine get settled today and while we were hemming a pair of curtains, who knocks on the door but a uniformed soldier! He had coppery-brown hair and I felt like I had seen him somewhere before. He said, "Good afternoon, Mrs. Harrison, I happened to be in town and thought I would pay you a social call, if that's all right." Catherine blushed prettily, and replied, "Oh, yes, Lieutenant Wainwright. Do come in. I'll make some tea." He sat down at the table and the two began to chat. Suddenly I had a feeling I was the third wheel on an apple cart. Later I went home and told Luke. He frowned, shook his head, and said, "I don't guess we're going to have a schoolteacher in Silverstone for very long after all."

Journal Entry: October 24, 1867

The most horrible thing occurred several weeks ago. Sheriff Montano came pounding at our door, saying he needed Luke's help because the Ames' place caught fire and it was likely that outlaws were responsible. The sheriff said, "I need another gun with me, amigo."

He went on to say he had heard Luke was a fast draw and a sharp shooter—something I did not know, and something from Luke's past he wanted desperately to forget. He had killed men in the war and vowed never to aim the barrel of a gun at another human being. However, I begged him to ride out with Sheriff Montano anyway, as I feared for the lives of the eight Ames children. Reluctantly he agreed and Sheriff Montano handed him a holster and ammunition belt, which he strapped around his waist. I took one look at the hard set to his shadowed jaw and the pistols at his hips, and decided he scarcely resembled my loving pastor-husband. Instead, he appeared more like a seasoned gunman. He said, "Beth, you get yourself down to the Bentleys and wait for me there." I obeyed at once, for it never even occurred to me to argue. There was something about this never-before-seen facet to my husband's character that almost frightened me, and yet I felt enveloped by a strong sense of security, too.

At the Bentleys' place, Adam, Charlotte, and I prayed until Luke returned. Finally around midnight I heard the rattling sound of an approaching wagon as its wheels crunched the rutty, stony terrain. I ran to the door and saw Luke with every one of the Ames kids in tow. They were frightened but unharmed. After we got home and settled the children into makeshift beds all around the cabin, Luke told me what happened.

Outlaws, indeed, had looted Ralph Ames' homestead. But seeing their approach, Warring Spirit hid the children down in the well behind the cabin. It is a miracle they did not drown. Reggie said she almost lost her hold on Lorena and Michael a few times, and Jesse kept little Jeb's head above water while the others clung tightly to his neck. The two older ones had saved the lives of their siblings and were utterly exhausted from their efforts.

Luke then informed me how he and the sheriff rode stealthily onto the Ames' property. From their undetected vantage point, they surveyed the gang, led by none other than Clayton Buchanan's foreman, Seth Patterson! They saw eight men, but Luke and Sheriff Montano made quick work of eliminating them. I told Luke he was brave and that I was proud of him, but he said he felt disgusted with himself for breaking his vow to the Lord. So I asked him, "King David did his share of killing the enemy. . .what is the difference in what you did?" Luke replied, "I don't know. It just makes me sick, is all."

Luke went on to say that once the outlaws were dead, he and the sheriff set out to inspect the damage. Mr. Ames' cabin had burned to the ground by then, and to their dismay, they discovered Warring Spirit had been killed. They also happened upon Ralph, who was mortally wounded yet still alive. Luke prayed with the man, after which Ralph said, "Your wife owes me. . .this is what I ask. . .that she raise my brood like her own." Luke gravely announced the children were nowhere to be found and that is when Ralph pointed to the well. With his dying breath, he said, "In there. In there."

Tears streamed down my face when Luke told me this. He gathered me onto his lap like a little girl, and I hung onto him and sobbed into his shoulder—for Ralph, for Warring Spirit, for eight children who no longer had parents.

Finally I lifted my head. "Luke," I said, "I am glad you killed those hateful men."

He did not say a word for a very long while. At last, he replied, "Reckon I didn't have much choice, Beth. If I hadn't taken their lives, they'd have moved on to another homestead, and what if that would have been Harlan's, or the Ramseys', the Bentleys'. . .or ours?"

I snuggled deeper into Luke's embrace and felt very safe in his arms.

So now Luke and I have eight children. By April, there will be nine. Just yesterday morning Luke said, "I have a feeling before long there'll be twenty kids running around this place." Upon hearing the remark, I suddenly felt very, very tired.

Journal Entry: December 27, 1867

I have never known a more joyous Christmas celebration than the one that took place in our very cabin two days ago. The Bentleys joined us and the children have taken to calling them "Granny" and "Gramps," which pleases the older couple no end. We sang and praised God for sending His only begotten Son to earth to save our souls and then we exchanged presents and ate beef stew and spice cake.

Luke surprised the children by producing two yellow-colored puppies. They were promptly named "Goldie" and "Sunshine," and they are the cutest, fattest, cuddliest little things I have ever laid eyes on. Luke said the pups will keep the younger children occupied while the older ones are at school. I know he is right.

Journal Entry: February 6, 1868

I can scarcely believe the news I heard today. Luke came home from town and said Millie Baker ran off with a soldier-friend of Lieutenant Wainwright, the gentleman courting Catherine Harrison. Luke said Mrs. Baker has been crying for hours and Mr. Baker is as mad as a raging bull. Lieutenant Wainwright and Sheriff Montano took off after the couple, but Luke said if Millie and that soldier do not want to be found, it is likely they will not be. However, that soldier is liable to be court-martialed. I only pray Mr. Baker does not get a hold of him first!

Journal Entry: April 2, 1868

Joshua Luke McCabe came into the world very early this morning. I had a very easy time of delivering him, and he is the most perfect child I have ever seen. He is fair-headed with cobalt-blue eyes and I think he favors the McCabes.

My dear sister-in-law Grace has been with me for the past week and has been a tremendous help with the children. She is also a nurse and assisted me in the birthing process, although she claims her presence was unnecessary.

Luke is the proudest papa in all of the Arizona Territory. Upon learning I bore him a son, he burst into our cabin and *kissed me until I could not breathe. Then he carefully took Joshua into his arms and is presently sitting in the rocking chair with him. Luke's misty gaze is fixed on our baby, and I can tell he is praising the Lord, just as I am. Our other eight children are at the Bentleys, but they will be returning shortly. They are almost as excited about Joshua's arrival as Luke!*

I am the luckiest woman on earth. I have a husband who loves me and nine precious children. I have the Bentleys who are as caring as my own parents and a Savior in Heaven who guides my every step.

Dearest Lord, I do thank You for bestowing such blessings upon me. I have done nothing to deserve all You have given me. You are a great God and I shall forever praise Your name. Though the trials are sure to come, my faith in You shall remain undaunted!

A Letter To Our Readers

Dear Reader:

In order that we might better contribute to your reading enjoyment, we would appreciate your taking a few minutes to respond to the following questions. We welcome your comments and read each form and letter we receive. When completed, please return to the following:

Rebecca Germany, Fiction Editor
Heartsong Presents
PO Box 719
Uhrichsville, Ohio 44683

1. Did you enjoy reading *An Undaunted Faith?*
   ❑ Very much. I would like to see more books
      by this author!
   ❑ Moderately
      I would have enjoyed it more if _____
      _____
      _____

2. Are you a member of **Heartsong Presents**? Yes ❑ No ❑
   If no, where did you purchase this book? _____
   _____

3. How would you rate, on a scale from 1 (poor) to 5 (superior), the cover design? _____

4. On a scale from 1 (poor) to 10 (superior), please rate the following elements.

   _____ Heroine   _____ Plot

   _____ Hero   _____ Inspirational theme

   _____ Setting   _____ Secondary characters

5. These characters were special because_____

_____

_____

6. How has this book inspired your life?_____

_____

_____

7. What settings would you like to see covered in future
   Heartsong Presents books?_____

_____

_____

8. What are some inspirational themes you would like to see
   treated in future books?_____

_____

_____

9. Would you be interested in reading other **Heartsong
   Presents** titles?   Yes ❑   No ❑

10. Please check your age range:
    ❑ Under 18   ❑ 18-24   ❑ 25-34
    ❑ 35-45   ❑ 46-55   ❑ Over 55

11. How many hours per week do you read?_____

Name _____

Occupation _____

Address _____

City _____ State _____ Zip _____

new year, new love

Introducing four brand-new novellas in modern settings that reflect on the anticipation of entering a new year—new calendar, new goals to accomplish, and a new chance at love. Rejoice in the transformation of a young woman in *Remaking Meridith* by Carol Cox. Throughout *Beginnings*, Peggy Darty will have you laughing and crying as two lonely adults are laid up in the hospital over the holiday season. Then, discover how setting goals brings together a church singles' class and sparks the flame of love in *Never Say Never* by Yvonne Lehman. Finally, in *Letters to Timothy*, see how author Pamela Kaye Tracy unites five needy people with one pen pal letter.

paperback, 352 pages, 5 ¾₆" x 8"

❤ ❤ ❤ ❤ ❤ ❤ ❤ ❤ ❤ ❤ ❤ ❤ ❤ ❤ ❤ ❤ ❤

❤ ❤ ❤ ❤ ❤ ❤ ❤ ❤ ❤ ❤ ❤ ❤ ❤ ❤ ❤ ❤ ❤

·····Hearts♥ng·····

·······Presents·······

Great Inspirational Romance at a Great Price!

Heartsong Presents books are inspirational romances in contemporary and historical settings, designed to give you an enjoyable, spirit-lifting reading experience. You can choose wonderfully written titles from some of today's best authors like Peggy Darty, Sally Laity, Tracie Peterson, Colleen L. Reece, Lauraine Snelling, and many others.

When ordering quantities less than twelve, above titles are $2.95 each.
Not all titles may be available at time of order.

Hearts♥ng Presents
Love Stories Are Rated G!

That's for godly, gratifying, and of course, great! If you love a thrilling love story, but don't appreciate the sordidness of some popular paperback romances, **Heartsong Presents** is for you. In fact, **Heartsong Presents** is the *only inspirational romance book club*, the only one featuring love stories where Christian faith is the primary ingredient in a marriage relationship.

Sign up today to receive your first set of four, never before published Christian romances. Send no money now; you will receive a bill with the first shipment. You may cancel at any time without obligation, and if you aren't completely satisfied with any selection, you may return the books for an immediate refund!

Imagine. . .four new romances every four weeks—two historical, two contemporary—with men and women like you who long to meet the one God has chosen as the love of their lives. . .all for the low price of $9.97 postpaid.

To join, simply complete the coupon below and mail to the address provided. **Heartsong Presents** romances are rated G for another reason: They'll arrive *Godspeed!*